The Game Ain't Nothin' but a Shame

The Game Aint Nothin' but a Shame

Ruff Lyfe

308 North Aster Ave.

Broken Arrow, Ok 74012

The Game Aint Nothin' But a Shame Copyright © 2021 by Ruff Lyfe

All rights reserved. No parts of this book may be reproduced in any form or by any means without prior consent of the Publisher, except brief quotes used in reviews.

ISBN-9798587397569
$15.00 USD
View on Amazon

Disclaimer:

This is a work of fiction. Any references or similarities to actual events, real people, living or dead, or to real locals are intended to give the novel a sense of reality. Any similarity in other names, characters, places, and incidents is entirely coincidental.

About the Author

Author Ruff Lyfe, born Charles Edwin Ruffin is an American author, recording artist and entrepreneur. Ruff Lyfe is from Muskogee Oklahoma and has three kids. He has been In and out of incarceration since the age of fifteen and into his thirties. Despite the hard times and struggles that he has faced, he continues to push for greatness. Ruff Lyfe refuses to let his past mistakes keep him from the destiny and purpose God has for him.

Connect With The Author:

www.facebook.com/charlesruffin87

www.instagram.com/rufflyfe87

www.twitter.com/rufflyfe87

Dedication

My first and foremost dedication is to God! Jesus Christ! If it wasn't for you keeping me under your mighty wings then I would not be here! It's only because of you God that I have not lost my mind and that I'm still alive. Thank you God for choosing me to be the one to break generational curses!

I dedicate this book to my family! Family First baby we did it! I dedicate this book to all the ones who have ever believed in me. I dedicate this book to everyone who has put up with my consistent talk about this book and even read it in its sloppy handwritten form. I dedicate this book to the unknown authors who encouraged me to continue writing and finishing this book. I dedicate this book to my friend that first typed this book up for me and edited it into its manuscript form.

I dedicate this book to all the people who have ever had a dream and have been scared to chase after it. I dedicate this to you because if I can do it then I believe that anybody can do it. I dedicate this book to all the people in the world that are locked up and away from their families. I feel your pain! I feel your struggles!

I dedicate this book to all the naysayers that said I would never do anything with my life. I dedicate this book to you because I want you to know that a person's past does not determine their future. I dedicate this book to the one plotting suicide to tell you that you have a purpose. I'm writing this book to not only inspire one person but to inspire generations to come that if you put your mind to it then you can achieve whatever you set out to do. It's not how you start the race but how you end. Continue to push past self doubt and all negative energy.

I dedicate this book to you (yes you) that have this book in your hand. I dedicate this book to you because you are special and you have a purpose in your life. Do not let the enemy have the final say so, because he is a defeated foe! Believe in yourself and refuse to give up on your dreams in life. It's not too late because you have breath! Now breathe new life into whatever that has been stagnant.

"Nothing is set in stone unless it is written on our headstone…"

Author Unknown

"When moving out the way of yourself will cause you to succeed in life, when will you choose to move out the way? You have a choice and if you continue to make the same decisions that lead you to destruction, but want someone to be sorry for you then you are a fool. Don't be a fool my friend! If you're breathing it's not too late! I believe in you!"

Author Ruff Lyfe

Prologue

Man, I ain't with the stupidity or nonsense anymore. I'm too old to be a crash dummy. I've spent my whole life so far, basically, trying to live up to others expectations but not no more. From this day forward, I'ma live the life I know I should live and that's just bein' real with myself.

I believe that God has a purpose for me here on this earth. Although I'm not exactly sure what it is, I do know for sure it's not to be a hardcore gangbanger, king pin drug dealer, jack boy, or player-player for the rest of my life.

I've been in and outta jails and institutions since fifteen years old. Honestly, I'm fed up of this continual vicious cycle over and over again which never seems to end. Therefore, today I'm making a conscious decision to break this cycle.

Currently, I'm twenty-seven years old serving this eight year sentence and I've been in this time since age twenty-four. I have less than a year to go before I discharge and I know that in order to stay free this time when I'm released I have got to plan ahead and have a vision. I have got to get serious about God and allow Him to transform me by the renewing of my mind because I now finally realize that I can do nothing good by myself. I know now, I need God.

I have to stop simply going through the motions pretending to have it all figured out when in reality I'm in desperate need of direction and help. I'm sick and tired of going through this same ol' bull.

My drug and alcohol addiction have a control over me although I barely admit it. I usually pretend I have it in control and I only do it for fun. Well, it's not fun anymore because it continues to take my freedom away from me.

It's not only my drug and alcohol addiction but also the fast money addiction that keeps me one foot in the game and one foot out the game. I say one foot in and one foot out because I know that I shouldn't be doing any illegal activity because I know it's wrong. Then again, it's too easy to make some quick money so I don't have to be broke.

I never wanted to stay in the game forever anyway. I just wanted to stack up enough money where I could turn it all into legal businesses, real estate and stuff like that. But all this stuff keeps pushing me further and further away from my wife and two kids because I'm not present in their lives.

I am the big A, which means I'm absent from their lives. I learned about the Big A from Worley Holman who teaches Inside Out Dad here in prison. He speaks about it often, saying we can't try to run or control people when we're absentees.

All I can say is, "boy oh boy, I'm tired of being the Big A."

Chapter One

"Ruff Dawg, Ruff Diggedy Dawg," I heard someone screamin' out my name. I looked up and it was T.

"What's up wit it, dawg?" I said, noticing his facial expressions which read something was going on.

"Man, you ain't heard about Bozo? He just got took out on a stretcher. He passed out and had a seizure. You know yesterday they took him to court because they say he was seen comin' out the shower at two in the mornin' with a peezy."

"Yeah, bro, that's crazy," I said. "I hope he gone be alright, though."

"Man, I do too," T said enthusiastically. "The chief of security said he has a fractured jaw and blood on his brain. They sayin' he might not live from all the swelling. They just put Red in jail and they lookin' fo' YG right now."

"Dang, man. Well I'ma keep 'em all in prayer because that's some serious stuff."

"Mos def," T replied.

"Well dawg, I gotta get over to this class so I will bark back at you."

"It's on."

That's crazy what happened to Bozo, I'm thinking to myself while sittin' in this boring class I'm in. If it ain't one thing it's always another in this joint. I will be glad to be up and outta here and to stay outta here this time for good. Jails and prison ain't for me even though this is my second time coming through Lexington A&R. I don't see myself as a bad individual although I continue getting locked up like I'm one. What is wrong with me that I can't seem to stay outta lock up and keep my freedom?

"Ruff, you aiight over there?" Tiger hollered from across the room.

"Yeah, I'm good bro. Just sittin' here thinkin' to myself."

"That's what up. I seen you was stuck in a daze so I was just checkin' on you."

"Yeap, yeap," I said.

Tiger was alright. He's twenty-five from Thug Town and reps 107 Hoover Crip. When I first got to this yard last year he was one of the first people I met because he was a cell over from mine. We usually linked up together to play basketball and that brought us closer as homeboys.

When I first met Tiger he was into church and reading his bible tough which convicted me that I needed to get back in my Word like I know I should. Now, Tiger has become bitter and vengeful because he did not get his GED that the judge said he needed before he went back to court. Also, Tiger just lost his dad a month or two ago so he's still recovering from that. To cope he has started smoking weed again.

"Hello! What's up Nelle?" I said as I heard her voice on the other end of the phone.

"Nothin'. Sittin' at the house, bored," she said.

"Oh, that's what's up. Well, have you been doin' okay today?"

"Yeah, I guess."

"Well, that's good. Where the kids?" I said.

"They right here. Here, y'all daddy wanna talk to y'all."

"Hi Daddy?"

"Hello baby, what you doing?"

"Nothin', just got through eatin' and we went to daycare today, too."

"Oh, that's good Charliah. Did you have fun?"

"Yes, we had fun and we went outside and I played with my friends, too."

"Well, that sounds like a lotta fun."

"It was."

"Well, Charliah, I love you and I miss you."

"I love you and miss you, too, Daddy. Here, Charles," my daughter said.

"Hi Daddy!"

"Hey Charles, what you up to?"

"Nothin'," he said sharply.

"Have you been being a big boy?"

"Yes."

"Well, be good, son. I love you and miss you."

"I love and miss you, too."

"Okay, put yo' momma back on the phone."

"Here, Momma. Daddy wants you."

"What you bout to be doin', Nelle?"

"Nothin'. Ain't got no money to do nothin'. All I do is work and come home," she lied.

"Yeah, I'm sure you do," I said while changing the conversation. "Why ain't you wrote me a letter?"

"I've been busy with work and takin' Charles to football practice and when I get through with all that I be tired. You know I don't like writing anyway."

"Yeah, but you told me you were and still ain't did it Nelle. Why you be doin' me like that?"

"Ain't nobody doin' you like nothin'," she snapped. "I said I'ma do it so stop rushing me and wait."

"Yeah, well you say it but actions speak louder than words."

"You gone get one," Nelle screamed as the operator interrupts, *you have sixty seconds remaining.*

"Well, I'm just gone stop asking because it seems useless. We have sixty seconds left so—it was good talking to you. I love you and miss you."

"It was good talking to you too. I love you and miss you, too."

"Aiight then Nelle. Later."

"Later," she said as the phone cut off.

"You know, I'm tired of my wife slow playin' me bout sending me a letter homie. It ain't about the letter, but it's about sacrifice, commitment, loyalty, and to me if she can't do somethin' that small, then I feel like I'm wasting my time with her. She aint wrote a nigga in over four month's dawg."

"Yeah, I feel you," T said. "I was telling my wife the same thing. She suppose to have sent me a letter last month and I still ain't got it."

"It's crazy, ain't it dawg," I said as my attention got drew to the dayroom where a fight had broken out.

At first I couldn't see who it was but as I got closer I seen it was Tiger who had the dude on the ground punching his face in. At this time I'm not knowing what's going on or none of that but later on Tiger told me that the dude kept playin' him outta five dollas that he owed him for the last month. He said when he asked dude about it he got to poppin' so he lost it and hopped on him. I told him I understood then kept it pushin'.

Tiger was five foot four inches tall, light skinned, with short hair. He usually kept a fade and he claimed to have 360 waves but all he had was a few waves on the side of his head. Tiger was a cool lil' dude but he had little man syndrome, bad. He believed no one could mess with him from the shoulders. He says all he has to do is hit em in the right spot. *The bigger they are, the harder they fall*, he'd always say.

"Yard's open!" the guard shouted over the loud speaker. Everyone is going in and out of the pod now. I filled up my cup with ice water and as much as I didn't want to work out today, I headed outside to meet T. T is forty years old, an O.G. from Piru, but he ain't into all the nonsense anymore. Weighing in at 225 pounds, he is what looks like pure muscle but he has a stomach on him. He works out doing something at least five days a week. We are both from Muskogee, plus we knew each other on the streets so we clique very well together. On top of that, he stays in his Word and encourages me to do the same thing.

"What took you so long to get out here," T said as I got to the ballfield to workout with him.

"Shoot, bro. The yard *just* opened," I responded.

"I know, homie," T spoke playfully while smiling and bouncing his chest muscles up and down. "I gotta keep you motivated lil' bro. No hurt, no big shirt. You see it."

"C'mon man. What we gone do today?" I say.

"Today is push-ups; all push-ups. Start out with fifty on the first one, then we gone do a hundred. After that, we gone do ten sets of fifty. That will be 650 push-ups."

"It's on," I say as I take my shirt off and flex. "It's nothin' to a boss, dawg. No hurt no big shirt." I stretch my arms then get down and knock out fifty quickly.

"Good money," T complimented then hopped down and done 100 push-ups without stopping.

"Man, why didn't you do yo fifty?" I said.

"I did it before you got here, homie."

Aiight, let me knock this hun-dun out right quick." I did seventy-five push-ups then got up, stretched, then dropped back down to finish the twenty-five push-ups I had left.

"Ruff, I been praying for you a lot lately. I mean I pray for everybody, but lately God has been placing it on my heart to pray for you continuously. I been praying for you and your wife and also that God's will be done in y'all's life. I believe and have faith that God is gone do tremendous things in your life. I want to encourage you to keep going forward no matter what the situation looks like. God is still on the throne; therefore He will make a way out of no way. As long as we trust in Him, He will take us from faith-to-faith, glory-to-glory.

"Yeah, you right T," I said. "I've been in and outta this lock-up too many times and to continue doing the same thing over and over expecting different results is insanity. My heart used to be into gangbangin' but not no more. What has gangbanging done for me? Nothing at all."

All this homie-this and homie-that stuff, I'm really tired of it. I mean I really don't even mess with all the so-called homies like that and it's because we ain't on the same mission. I mess with anybody rather Blood, Crip, GD, white, Mexican, black, or whatever. As long as we got the same mission and the same focus then we can kick it.

Before I'm anything, I'm a man and as a man there is certain stuff that we have to let go of. In the Bible it even says, 'When I was a child I thought like a child, but when I became a man I put away childish things,' or somethin' like that.

I know I have a long way to go but I've came a long way as well. I thank God for blessing me continuously and keeping me away from hurt, harm and danger. He has been too good to me is what I'm basically saying. If it's a choice between Christian and gangbangin', then I'm Christian all day.

Man, now it's August and I got five months until I'm outta this hell-hold. These last few months done shot by. I finish Inside Out Dad this month and the S.A.T. program next month. Therefore, I'm just staying busy 'cause January 2015 is my year. That's why I'm taking all the classes and programs that I can. I even take some programs that don't give me any days.

It's all good though because I take programs for the knowledge. We perish because of lack of knowledge. I remember back when I was younger I heard an Old School kat say that white folks would say that if they didn't want black folks to know somethin' then they would put it in a book. That's because they say we would never read it.

As cold as that may sound, it's got half-truth in it. The full truth of the matter is it ain't just blacks but all races, nowadays. Anyways, while I'm in here I'm just tryna learn as much as possible. I know its crunch time in my life so I gotta buckle down on a lotta stuff in order to be productive. Real talk, I'm not tryina come back here no more. I want to keep my freedom forever. No more jail cells or penitentiary yards.

Chapter 2

I don't know how things gonna work out with me and my wife, Nelle. We been together since 2005 and got married in 2008 while I was locked up in county jail awaiting prison for the second time. The first time I didn't go—I had a four month review and got out. I was sentenced to the RID program, *balance suspended on completion*. That time I did seven months; three months before I signed and then four months after, then I was released on five years probation. Nelle and I actually got together on that bid I was doing. I was still seventeen and me and a few potnas mess around and got locked up on a burglary in the 2nd degree charge. It was June 21st 2005 and I was just sitting at the house writin' rhymes and was fixin' to blow an L. I gotta rang on my cellphone and it was Jo-Jo.

"What up, Ruff? I was tryna see if you know were a lick was at. I'm wit A-City and we bout to swang through."

"Aiight, bet. I know one lil' place we can check out but besides that I don't even know. But it's on," I said.

Jo-Jo replied, "It's on," then hung up the phone.

I know I didn't need to be hittin' no lick because I just got out of Rader. It's really called Lloyd E. Rader detention center and is located in Sand Springs, Oklahoma.

21

That's where they sent juvenile delinquents and youthful offenders. The kids there had crimes ranging from burglary to robbery, arson to kidnapping, rape to murder and all in between. I had just got out of Rader on February 10th 2005. I had just got off probation on June 10th 2005 because on June 27th I was gone be eighteen years old. Well, I got jammed up that 21st day of June.
busted by the cops

A-City and Jo-Jo pulled up outside the house in a little red Ford Corolla with four doors. I got off the couch and headed outside to chop it up with them.
Talk - shoot the breeze

"What up dawg? You ready?"

"You know I'm ready. I'm always down to ride," I say while lookin' at A City, which I really did not know.

Jo-Jo said, "Homie, this A-City I was tellin' you I was with. He a real nigga from Tulsa. He from 107 Hoover Crip."

"Okay, that's what up. What's good, bro?"

"I'm good," A-City replies while rubbing his hands together.

"I'm ready to go an' get this bread," Jo-Jo said. "Now where did you say was a lick?"

"Well, I heard ol' girl Susan's grand mmma be keepin' money ova there and could be a easy lick so we can go check it out, homie. Let me close the door to the house and we can ride out."

"Bet that," both Jo-Jo and A-City said at the same time while getting back in the red Corolla that they pulled up in.

"I got this blunt that we can smoke when we get back." I'm sittin' in the backseat, bobbin' my head to a Z-

22

Ro song. *Every day I'm still going through the same thang, I try so hard just to maintain, I'm real but people still talk down on my name...* "Turn right on Jefferson Street, bro."

"Bet," A-City said while turning down the volume to listen closely at what I was sayin.

"Y'all see that house right there on the corner. Well, that's Susan an' dem's house, but it's some van out there that look like an electric company or something. Whatever it is, we can't do this lick right now."

"What's up now?" Jo-Jo said.

"I don't know homie. This was the only thang I knew would be pretty easy." We kept driving for about five more minutes then A-City pulled up at some house off York and Gibson Street.

He said, "I'll be back."

"What is this nigga doin'?" I said.

"Ain't no tellin'," Jo-Jo responded.

We are sittin' in the driveway of somebody's house. A-City is knockin' on the front door; now the side door. He turns backwards and kicks the side door into this house.

"Come on, dawg. Let's go see what up," I said to Jo-Jo, seeing that A-City was already in this house.

As we entered into the house, A-City had the computer that he had wanted me and Jo-Jo to put in the car. We started takin' the computer out together to put in the car when we noticed a white woman lookin' in our direction with a phone to her ear.

I said, "Let's act like we live here and go ahead and put this computer in the car, then let bro know that it's time to ride out." After we put the computer in the car, we both run back into the house. "A-City! C'mon, it's a woman callin' the police right now."

Me and Jo-Jo head back to the car. I get in on the passenger side this time and Jo-Jo gets in the back.

What is takin' so long? A-City come runnin' out with two shotguns that he threw in the backseat, then hopped in the car and we smashed off. We put on our seatbelts, tryna act normal.

"There's uh chump, right there," Jo-Jo said. [police]

"Yeah, I see mayne. [man?] We need to jump outta here 'cause I ain't tryna be jammed up"

That police kept passin us so we were hoping we were cool. Less than thirty seconds later that same police is flying back our way. Ahead of us at the stoplight on Shawnee there's a few police. The police waited til we turned, then put his lights on.

"Smash on 'em, smash on 'em," I said.

"We gotta get out somewhere," Jo-Jo said.

A-City was lookin' in the rearview mirror, driving fast as possible in the lil' Corolla we were in. Now, I'd say it was thirty Muskogee police on our bumper. All the cars on the highway are parked to the side because they see the pursuit. A-City switches lanes driving on the wrong side of the highway. Some more police were standing with shotguns pointed at us. I don't know if A-City was tryna kill us or what cause he turned left into the side of the lane and we hit something that's supposed to stop cars from going past that point but at the speed we were going we hit the thing—BOOM!!!—the car rolled four or five times before landing in a small creek on all four tires. Lasers are on us. *Put your hands up! Put your hands up! KEEP 'EM UP! Put your hands out the window!* the police were screaming with shotguns and hand pistols all on us. Police grab us out through the windows which were all broken.

"What were you idiots doing? Y'all could've killed yourself and others doing this stupid stuff," one police said in an angry but concerned type of way as he puts the cuffs on me and walk me to the back of his police car where he begins to pat me down. "Do you got any knives or sharp objects in your pockets?"

"Naw," I said while lookin' at the highway and seeing cars passing by and people lookin' over in this direction because they want to know what's going on. "Be easy on my shoulder," I said. I was hurting badly there from the wreck. I believed it must have got bruised. The police put me in the backseat of the car.

I seen Jo-Jo get put in the police car ahead of me but have not seen A-City. It's police galore in this area right now, too. I look back and see about eight of the police together talkin' about what had to been this wreck because they were hyped up. One had his hands in the air demonstrating how the car hit the curb and started flipping.

All I kept thinking is *why did I choose to come hit a lick with these dudes?* I was sittin' at the house chillin' and Jo-Jo called me with this bull. Now I'm headed back to lock-up; back to orange jumpsuits; back to chow time and commissary and all the jail house blues. Man, if I would've just chilled, I wouldn't even be here right now. I ain't been out nothin' but four months and already headed back.

The police opened the back door to let me out of his patrol car. We were in the sally port of Muskogee County Detention Center. The police takes me to the police department to ask me questions. "What's your name?" he said.

"Charles Ruffin," I said while noticing his badge name which said Officer Todd Tilman. Officer Tilman could not have been older than thirty. He was white with no facial hair except for his eyebrows which were black and bushy. His bald head was shining as if he had put some grease on it that morning.

"How old are you?"

"Seventeen."

"Date of birth?"

"Six. Twenty-seven. Eighty-seven."

"So, you're about to have a birthday in a couple of days, I see."

"Yeap."

Officer Tilman scratched his right ear then looked me dead in the eyes. "Mr. Ruffin, what were y'all thinkin'? Don't you know y'all could've killed yourselves or someone else the way y'all were driving that car?"

"Yeah, I know," I said while thinking hell I anit the one who was driving but I knew what he meant.

"Let me uncuff one of your hands so I can fingerprint you. Ima take your picture and then take you over to the jail."

This police looked like he had been lifting weights for a couple of years because his bicep muscles were bulging outta the sleeve of his shirt. He had me hold some card thing with some numbers on it and had me take two pictures. One was facing straight forward and the other one was facing to the side. "That's all," Officer Tilman said as he grabbed the card I was holding, then says, "Let me put the other cuff back on you, then take you over to the jail."

Chapter Three

As we entered into the back sally port gate into the jail my stomach was in disgust. It was jailers standing waiting on me who said, "Face the wall on the right." The police was uncuffing me while I heard the guards sayin', "That's the juvenile who was in the high speed chase. The other two adults will be here at any moment."

"Put your hands on the wall," a chubby short black guard said as he began to pat search me for any drugs, weapons, or contraband. "Take everything out our pockets and put it in the bucket."

"Be easy on my shoulder," I said. "It hurts real badly and I'm in pain."

The guard touched it and I squirmed down. He asked did I want to go to the hospital so I said, *Yeah*. Really I just wanted to prolong the jail stay, again.

Officer Tilman was still standing there so he volunteered to take me to the hospital. <u>I still had on my all-black Nike Air Max shoes.</u> The guard never told me to take them off so I didn't.

Officer Tilman said, "Put your hands in front of you and I will cuff you up." He cuffed me up then starts walking me back to his patrol car, saying loudly, "Officer out the back!"

The metal sliding door opened up. I see two police bringing in A-City who looked like he had been wooped on by the police. There was bleeding off the side of his head and his eyes were closed like he had got sprayed with some mace. His shirt was torn up with blood on it. He was mumbling something I couldn't understand. On the way to the hospital I was thinkin', *why did they do him like that?* I did not know A-City, but I still did not like the fact that the police did him like that.

We pulled up to the hospital and I seen my momma and my sister Nicole standin' there crying. The police was walking me into the emergency room and I told them, "I'm okay. My shoulder is just bruised up a little."

I don't know how they heard about all this but in Muskogee word travels quick. We stopped at a glass window where there was an older white woman around the age of fifty-five. She told me, "Have a seat so I can ask you a few questions."

"Okay," I said and she asked me my name, birthday, social security number, and did I have insurance; all that stuff. When I said I didn't have insurance, she looked at me with a lil' smirk.

She said, "Mr. Ruffin, what is wrong with you?"

"I just had a car wreck and my shoulder is in intense pain."

"Okay. Go through the door on the right, then take a left and the last door on the left go inside and a nurse will be in there shortly."

A short but thick light-skinned female came in; who I figured was the nurse. Her scrubs were fitting her tight, making all her body curves exposed. Her hair was flat-ironed to the side which was down to her shoulder. As her green eyes connected with my brown eyes, I licked my lips and smiled.

"How are you?" she said.

"Fine. And you?" I said while imagining licking all the lip gloss off her lips and my eyes had her undressed completely. Those nice round shaped breast had my eyes glued as she was leaning over to pick up a pen that she'd dropped on the floor. I could've sworn she dropped that pen on purpose just so she could tease a brother.

She said, "My name is Lovely and I'm your nurse for today."

She asked me what was wrong and I told her about my shoulder. Officer Tilman was standing with his arms folded like he was just ready to leave. The nurse checked my blood pressure and heartrate. Her perfume was smellin' like a scratch-n-sniff pull out in a magazine or at least that's what it seemed like because that's all my nose could smell. Not to mention, this woman was a ten on a scale of 1 to 10. Her black and pink air-brushed finger nails I couldn't help but notice as she pulls my left sleeve up to look at the bruise on my shoulder. Her hands were soft and warm. She grabbed an alcohol swab and rubbed it on the bruise as my face frowned up in pain. She put some triple antibiotic ointment on it and then puts a big bandage on it.

"I think you're gone be okay," she said while turning toward Officer Tilman. "I'm through with him," she said while walking out the door.

Shakin' my head as I look at that fat, juicy booty— *She gotta know what she doin'*, I'm thinkin' to myself.

"Let's go Mr. Ruffin," Officer Tilman said.

We head out the same way we came in. I see my momma and sister sittin' in the waitin' room as we exit the first door.

"You okay?" momma said.

"Yeah, I'm okay."

"Okay. I love you. Keep yo' head up. We will be at court tomorrow."

"Okay, momma. Nicole. I love y'all too." Back at the jail I have to repeat the same ol' pat search stuff and get booked into the jail. I get uncuffed again by Officer Tilman and then he leaves out the back gate.

"Go in there and have a seat," the chubby guard told me, "then I will be with you to take your picture, change you out, and send you to South Detox where the juvenile pod is."

"Aiight," I said as if this was my first merry-go-round.

"Ruffin," a different guard called my name. This one was dressed in Sheriff's clothes so I figured he had a little bit more rank. He told me he had to ask me some questions and it would only take a few minutes. This guard was tall and skinny with a military cut. He had a thick mustache and I noticed a gold wedding band on his left finger which told me that he was married.

The cards were a few different colors which were basically saying what all I had on me, from clothes to shoes to other personal belongings. *Do I have any health problems? Am I a smoker? Do I have any tattoos?* After I finished that he told me to go over to the corner where there was a window and on the wall was a thing showing your height and I took a mugshot right there. Then he told me to give him my clothes and shoes. I take my shoes off, my pants off, and the black shirt off that I had on and put it in the window. He then gave me a 2X jumpsuit and a pair of orange shower shoes that I put on and then he took me to this lil' room where the fingerprint machine was and the O.S.B.I. computer thing.

"We're all through with this process," the guard said. "So, now I'm gone take you over to South Detox. Open One. Open South Detox!" the guard screamed loud and the loud clanging doors came open.

South Detox was small. It was only three cells in there, but they would still pack juveniles in there if they had to.

"Ruff Dawg, what's good, peep?"

"Ain't nothin', K.O.," I said while shakin' his hand with my right hand, giving him the Blood handshake. I hugged him with my left arm.

K.O. was Jo-Jo's younger brother. He was sixteen and in for shooting with intent to kill. K.O. was light-skinned, short, and stocky and looked just like Jo-Jo except Jo-Jo was taller than K.O. and also more thinner. Jo-Jo was nineteen years old and he had already been locked up two different times as a juvenile for armed robbery. In 2002 we were co-defendants on a robbery and that's how we got sent to Rader.

I told K.O. the whole scoop on what went down with me, Jo-Jo and A-City. I went to take a shower and then I called it a wrap because it was now 11:30 at night and I was tired as a slug.

"Rise and shine, it's breakfast time! Rise and shine, it's breakfast time! Rise and shine, it's breakfast time!"

A loud, obnoxious guard kept repeating this over the speakers which woke me up. *Why was this weirdo hollerin' if it ain't no chow out there?* I went ahead and hopped out of my bunk, brushed my teeth, washed my face with a cut up towel that I made a couple face cloths outta last night before I took a shower. I took a leak, washed my hands and went and sat at the table in the small dayroom.

I wonder what is this judge gone be talkin' 'bout today? I hope he talkin' 'bout a cheap bond cause my momma told me that if I got a bond then she would get me out. The bruise on my shoulder seemed to hurt even more than it did yesterday.

"Open South Detox! Chow time! Chow time!" the black guard said who had braids in his hair and was probably about six foot two inches tall and 215 pounds with a chin strap facial hair edge-up. He gave me a tray as I nodded my head what up to him and in return he nodded his head back, saying, "Last call fo' chow!"

I said my grace and knocked off the two boiled eggs that we had on the tray along with the grape jelly and two toast.

"Is it aiight if I grab one of these cups," I said to a dark-skinned dude who looked like I had known him from somewhere else.

"Go ahead, homie. That's what they there for," he said.

I grabbed me a cup and got some ice cold water out of the jug the guard brought.

"What up, homie?" I said to K.O. who looked still half asleep.

"Tryna finish this lil' bite, then go back to sleep, bro. It's too early for me, Ruff Dawg. That's what up."

"Even if I tried to, I know I'm gone be up all day."

The TV was on VH1 so I was listening to the top 20 Countdown when I heard, *Ruffin...Ruffin...* "What up?" I said while walking toward the speaker on the wall of the dayroom. *Call Nelle at her grandma's...* "Okay. I got it. Thanks."

I pick up the phone to make a collect call.

Press one for English; two for Spanish...

I press one, then the operator says *enter one, then the area code, then the seven digit number you would like to call...*

1-9-1-8-6-8-3-4-3-3-0...

Enter your inmate identification number after the tone... *tone...

4-4-6-7-2-3-5-4-4...

Your call is being connected...

ring... ring... ring...

"Hello?" I heard Nelle's voice say before the operator said, *this is Global Tellink. You have a collect call from "Ruff Dawg", an inmate in Muskogee County Jail... If you would like to accept this call, press five now... If you would like to block this and future collect calls, press nine now... This call may be subject to recording and monitoring... Thank you for using GTL...*

"Hello," I said.

"What's up with you?" replied Nelle.

"I'm just sittin here chillin'."

"Have you heard anything, yet?"

"Naw, not until I go to court at three."

"Well, me and Nicky will be there."

"Okay, bet," I said, thinkin' *what is Nelle got goin' on actin' like she my girl or somethin'?*

"Have you seen Jo-Jo or that otha dude that was with y'all?"

"I did yesterday, but I'm in the juvenile pod until I turn eighteen. I will see them at court when we go, though."

"You know, I was concerned about you, Charles when Nicky told me what had happened and I seen that lil' red car. It's all dented in with the windshield broken out. It looked like somebody would have died in a car like that."

"Yeah, I know," I said. "I thank God for keeping us safe. The only thing wrong with me is my shoulder is hurting a lil' bit, but besides that I'm good."

"I'm glad to hear that," Nelle said in a soft and innocent voice.

"That's sweet of you," I said as the operator interrupted me with the sixty second warning. "Well, it was good to talk to you," I said.

"It was good to talk to you, too," Nelle replied.

"Aiight, I'll get with you then, Nelle."

The phone hung up. Nicky was Jo-Jo's girlfriend and Nicky and Nelle were sisters. I've known Nicky for a while because we were both in the ninth grade together. When I got outta Rader, Nicky would tell me that I needah holler at her sister Nelle. I'm like, *I'm cool on all that* but one night me, Jo-Jo and Nicky and Nelle's brother Fast Freddy was on the back porch snortin' some lines and Nelle came in to meet me. She was lookin' good, her hair was braided up in a bun. She was dark chocolate and she was a few inches shorter than me. I'm 5' 6" tall so she is prolly 5' 3". Her eyes were sparkling along with the lip gloss she had on. I shook her hand and said, "I'm Charles," knowin she already knew my name.

"My name's Nelle," she said.

"Well, it's good to meet you," I said. " Hopefully we can chill sometimes."

It looked like Nelle and Nicky was going out or somethin' cause they had on dresses. Nelle was skinnier than Nicky. I really was not tryna mess with Nelle like that either. I was hopin' she couldn't tell that I was coked out.

Me and Jo-Jo kicked it tough every day, from smokin' weed, smokin' wett, poppin X pills, Xanax pills, or doing cocaine. When I got outta Rader, Jo-Jo was doing all these harder drugs and bein' my homeboy, he put me on to what he was doing and my addictive personality fell in love with it all.

Jo-Jo called me and told me that him, Nicky and Nelle were gone swang by for a minute. I said, *Bet* and twisted up a fat blunt and waited til' they pulled up. I sat there on the couch listening to music while thinkin' to myself, *what am I gone say to her?* This had to be the end of May 2005 when we first met.

"What up, Jo-Jo?" I said while taggin' him with the Blood sign. He hit me back up as I noticed Nelle had on some short shorts, a red shirt, and some red thongs on her feet. She had a beautiful smile and she showed her white teeth whenever she smiled.

"What up, Nicky? What up, Nelle?" I said as they both said Hi at what seemed to be the same time. "Let's get outta this heat," I said. "I got a blunt in here to blow, Jo-Jo, if you tryin' to."

[handwritten annotation: Joint]

"You already knowin' that, dawg."

"Already," I said while focusing my attention on Nelle who had her finger nails did, too!

Nelle is cool but she is too skinny fo' me I thought while grabbing the blunt off the table and firing it up. "Do you smoke, Nelle?"

"Nope," she said as she smiled and made a face that said, *Hell naw'll.*

"I was just askin', baby girl," I said while passin' the blunt to Jo-Jo.

"You cool, Charles. Ain't nothin' wrong with askin'."

"That's right," I said at the same time nodding my head in agreement with the statement I made.

"Here, Ruff Dawg!" Jo-Jo said, passin' the blunt back to me.

I was livin' with my sister Nicole at the time on 18th Street. She pulled up outside with her two kids, JJ and Kaury.

"My sister comin' in, y'all, so let's go out on the porch because she doesn't like me smokin' in the house. She prolly gone trip on me."

I turned the music off that was playin' that Boosie/Webbie, *Fo' yo daddy in the pen... Swerve on 'em... You ain't never had shit... Swerve on 'em...*

"What up, Nicole?" I said. She just looked at me wit uh look on her face like, *neegro please. You know better than that bullcrap. Don't say SHIT to me!* No, she didn't say it, but believe me she wanted to.

"Let me hit that one mo time Jo-Jo, before you throw it down." I took about three more puffs on the now dooby and then threw it on the ground. "What y'all got goin' on for later on?" I said.

"Shoot, prolly just maxin' and relaxin' with Nicky," Jo-Jo said while lookin' at her, which made Nicky smile.

Nicky was wearin' the same thing that Nelle was wearin' but Nicky had some fat titties and a fat booty to go with it. I don't be lookin' at her like that 'cause she the homie girl, but let's be real—it's hard not to notice.

"We 'bout to ride out," Jo-Jo said as him and Nicky started walking to Nicky's silver four-door Honda.

Nelle was lookin' back at me as she was makin' her way back to the car. Nelle waved her hand at me and said, "I will see you later."

"It's on," I said, turning around to go in the house.

"Sorry 'bout smoking in the house, Cole. I didn't know you were gone be home this early." That's what I call my sister Nicole for short.

"You know I told you 'bout smokin' in here, period, anyway," she said.

"I know and I'm sorry, like I said." Well, I usually said sorry all the time whenever I got caught smokin' in the house or she could smell it. I know she just put up with me because I was her brother and I know that bro could be somethin' else.

Chapter Four

Nelle came over the next day when I was at the house by myself. She called me and said she wanted to see me so I said *alright*, even though I really didn't care if she did or not. She was wearin' some capri pants, some all-white K-Swiss and a white t-shirt that said, "Look At Me!" in bold black letters. You know me, I was *definitely* lookin' at her, too.

"You lookin' good, lil' mama," I said while starin' in her eyes and putting out my right hand for her to grasp. As she grasped my hand, I pulled her close to me and gave her a big hug but a gentle kiss. The CD player was on O.G. Ron C Fuck Action 41: "We Belong Together"; *...Who am I gone lean on when times get rough?...Who's gone talk to me on the phone 'til the sun comes up?...who's gone take yo' place?... there ain't nobody else... Awww baby baby... we belong together...*

As we sit there on the couch noddin' our heads I place my arm around her waist and pull her closer to me. "Don't act like you scared of me," I said.

"I ain't," she said while scootin' closer to me, not in resistance to me pullin' on her.

My thoughts are runnin' rampant now. My hands fidgety and I could feel the X pill I took startin' to kick in on me, tough. I grab Nelle's left leg and put it over my right leg. I lick my lips at her and use my left hand to rub up and down on her inner thigh. My palms were sweaty, my teeth were grittin' and I was tryna knock somethin' right then. This was the first time me and Nelle had been alone by ourselves so I figure this was the best time to go ahead and make it happen.

Her legs were open so I go ahead and start feelin' on her coochie through her pants. She ain't stoppin' me either so now I'm tryna unbuckle her belt buckle. She just lookin' at me so I continue to unbuckle her belt. Now I unfasten her pants button and unzip her pants. I start suckin' on the left side of her neck while my left hand goes down her pants to where her coochie is. I got my hand on her panties though, usin' my fingers to rub in a circular motion. Her coochie is wet, too. I can feel it good through these silk black panties she got on. I get off the couch and get on my knees while pullin' her pants all the way down and she is helpin' me with it. She kicks one of her shoes off so that one pants leg she could take off. Now I'm pullin' off her panties. She has no coochie hair and a pearl tongue that literally looks like a lil' man on a boat. Her coochie lookin' edible, I wanted to eat it but wasn't into all that.

I had on some black basketball shorts so I pulled them down along with the boxers I had on. My dick rock hard, I lifted both her legs up and she kept them in that position for me while I held the base of my dick and put the head of it inside her, slowly. Lookin' in her eyes I could tell that she was ready for this dick. I pushed my dick harder inside her as she gasp for air and bit down on her lip at the same time.

Damn this feels good, I'm thinkin' while stroking deep inside of her slowly. Gradually I speed up tryna knock the bottom out of it. Her pussy muscles tightened around my dick as I rock the couch she is laying on. Her head steady wobbling against the pillow. Her eyes closed in amazement. She is biting down on her lower lip. I'm steady poundin' her coochie which is now wetter than an ocean. I swear she already done busted three nuts and I ain't even got off one yet.

"You got some good pussy, Nelle," I said; going faster than ever, makin' sho' she gets this entire dick.

I can feel a nut comin' on and I can tell that she is too because her legs are shiverin' and shakin' uncontrollably. My booty muscles tightened up. I'm goin' hard and sweatin' and I feel it comin' out but instead of pulling out, I keep goin'. My breathin' hard, my stroke's becoming shorter but harder than ever. I push my dick deep down inside of her as I bust all inside her and I know she is loving it because I can feel her steady grindin' on my dick.

I took my dick out of her, pulled my shorts and boxers up while lookin' at her facial expressions which said, *Damn nigga, you got some good dick.* She got up and put her leg back through her panties and pulled them up. She did the same with her pants, zipped them up, fastened them and tightened her belt buckle back in place. She put on her shoes, looked at the clock that was on the entertainment center which said 11:45 PM.

"Three hours passed by quick," Nelle said. "Shit, I gotta be to work tomorrow at five in the morning so I betta get goin'."

"It's on," I said while hugging her tightly and peckin' her on the lips then puttin' my tongue in her mouth as we begin French kissin'. I squeeze on her ass cheeks and pull her into this dick one last time before she heads out the door. "I'll holla at you."

"Bye," she replied.

***

Me and Nelle have been tight from the beginning but this incarceration she has fell off on me. I'm already knowin' that we will never be the same. I have less than a week before I discharge. I'm feelin' good, feelin' like there ain't nothin' can stop me. I have been keeping my faith in God that everything gone work out for the good. I pray that His will be done for my life as well as my wife's life. I really want to be with Nelle because I love her with all my heart. She really hurt me big time by jumpin' out the car on me for another man. The last time I was out I cheated on her, though, with two females. The thing about it is that they knew that they couldn't take my wife's place cause she been here fo' me from the start. I know that she loves me for me 'cause I ain't got no money. Matter fact, she probably should've left me a long time ago or we never should have even been and that's just real.

Today is January 14th 2015. I have exactly two days left and then I'm gone. I know that I am ready this time. I have a great support base and my attitude is God first and God's will in my life, not my own. My kids are older now. Well, they are six and seven which is still young but it's a crucial point in their lives where they need daddy there with them. I only been out basically one year of their life and that was last time when I got out in 2011. Therefore, this time I want to be the daddy to my kids that I should be. The daddy I'm talkin' about is a daddy that don't keep on getting locked up and being the Big A.

"Ruff Dawg. I needa holla at you when I get off work," T said as I was going through the line for dinner.

"It's on, bro. Fa-sho. Just holla at me, I'll be on the pod."

"Bet," T said.

I grabbed my tray, which was a hamburger patty, a roll, mashed potatoes, and Jell-O. I grab a spork then go take a seat by Brother Mack, one of the Christian brothers who was sitting by himself.

"What up, Mack?" I said.

"Knockin' this lil' ol' kids meal off so I can get back to the pod," he said.

"Same thing bro," I replied.

"Word is that you leavin' here in a couple days."

"Yeah, it's finally over wit," I said with a confident look on my face.

"Well, Ruff, I done seen you come a long way from when you first came in til now. And I want you to know this and really this ain't me talkin' but God talkin' through me when I say that God has big things in store for you. All you have to do is continue to keep Him number One priority in your life. For he knows the plans He has for you, plans to prosper you and not to harm you. Plans to give you a hope and a future. He said, 'Forget the former things, do not dwell on the past, for I am doing a new thing. Now that it springs up do you not perceive it? I am makin' a way in the desert and springs in the wasteland.'"

"That's real talk, homie," I said. "I thank you for giving me that Word from the Lord 'cause I know that's exactly where it came from. I know that He is steady working in my life and has brought me a long way. I should've been dead a long time ago but I'm still here so I know it's for a reason."

"Most definitely," Mack said as we both get up to leave.

Man, that's crazy I was sayin' to myself. Thinkin' bout the fact that I'm finally a short-timer. It seemed like this sentence would never end. I done nineteen months in the county befo' I pulled chains so imagine livin' like that. Yeah, it's crazy but you know what? *'All things work together for good to those who love Him and are called according to his purpose.'*

This time, I'm gone get out and stay out.

Fa sho'…

Chapter Five

Back on the pod I grab the remote and turn on the TV; turn to channel 3 which is Fox so I can catch the news. I sat down on this metal bunk bed, and then grabbed this book that I have a couple more chapters to read and then I'm done. It's called, "It's Your Time" by Joel Olsteen.

It's a pretty good book. I got faith and I claim it's my time, right now, in the name of Jesus. I'm thinkin' big thangs once I hit them streets. I know that God is on my side and I just read somewhere in the Bible—I forget the scripture—but it said, "Be bold and courageous. Do not be terrified. Do not be discouraged. For the LORD your God will be with you always."

I like to read books that are based on real stuff. What's that I think nonfiction, self-help books or books that can help me in some kind of way. I always gotta have the Living Word. The B-I-B-L-E. The Bible in which I've been making habit to read each and every day for at least the last past month and I go to church at least two times a week at the chapel.

My mind is everywhere right now so I can't read no book right now. I fold the tip of the page I was on and put it on the locker.

"What up?" T said.

"Chillin', chillin'," I said. "Lookin' at the weather on the news."

My celly wasn't in here at the time so he took his chair and sat in it.

"What I was talkin' 'bout was I'm tryna get that TV and J's you got when you leave," he said. "Naw'll, I'm just playin', but if God put it on yo' heart to give it to me, I will accept it, 'cause He know I need it. I got at least another six months up in here."

"You know what, bro? I just might do that for you 'cause I know how it is. I know first-hand so you already knowin' what up. I gotcha. You just continue to stay out the way like you know how to do. You know, if these people can keep us longer then they will."

"No bull. Well, Ima push back to my unit be fo' they lock these doors. God bless you," T said.

"God bless you, too," I said watchin' T hurry up outta here.

I lay back on the bed, close my eyes and I think, *How is thangs gone be with me and ol' Nelle this time?* As for the kids, I'm gone always take care of them cause one thang I ain't and won't be is a deadbeat dad. I will always take care of mine. Bottom line.

Sometimes I be thinkin', *why did I get married at such an early age?* Not sayin' it's a bad thang. I just be thinkin' 'cause twenty-one was kind of young. On top of that, I know I wasn't truly ready. Sometimes I wonder, *is this the woman God wants me with?* Everything tells me, *Yeah.* I can remember when I was younger, I prayed to God asking Him to send me a woman who loved me for me and we could be together forever. The way Nelle showed so much interest and love for me in the beginning, I knew she had to be the one. She would do anything that Charles said, too. Really she just wanted to please me and make me happy. I have to admit, that's one thang I loved about her, too.

Charles Jr. and Charliah mean everything to me. I sometimes think that they don't respect me as their father but I can't be mad when I ain't been in their life like I suppose to. I ain't seen them in over eight months, now. When Nelle jumped out the car in April 2014, she stopped writing me, she stopped visiting me, she stopped sending me money, and she stopped putting time on the phone.

I asked her to send me some pictures of the kids but she's always too busy or she ain't got no money or some lame excuse is all I get. She tells me nothing's changed but she just ain't had the money to come visit and this and that.

One thing I don't like is when Nelle wants to throw our kids in my face, sayin' *you ain't been here for them. I done did it all by myself the whole seven years. You was only here one year,* she always says. *I don't want you to hurt me or break my heart again.* She acts like what she does to me ain't nothin' to me.

I communicate wit' Nelle and keep it one hunnerd wit' her but she too blind or too ignorant to even notice that she gotta Real One. Even though I be gettin' locked up a lot doesn't make me a bad dude and if I'm that bad, then why has she been with me for nearly ten years? Honestly, Nelle has lost respect for me and I can tell it by the way she talks to me. I mean, even though we are married, it's not like we are even friends. I want to have a wife who is also my best friend. If I can tell somebody else somethin' then why couldn't I tell my wife? She doesn't communicate with me like I would like her to and I let her know this but nothing changes.

Here I am, about to be getting out again and really don't know where I'm even gone stay for sure. I have a few options as of right now, though. Most likely, off the top, I will go live with my momma. I know momma will always accept me and she always has. Me and my momma have a good relationship. I thank God for my momma. She is one who I can talk to about anythang.

I pray for her all the time, because God knows I don't want nothing bad to happen to her. I know that we as humans have to die but I don't want that to be the end of it. I want us to live together forever in heaven for eternity.

My daddy died in 1992. I tend to wonder how things would have been for me if he would have still been alive. It is what it is, though. I know all things happen for a reason. Everyone says I look just like my daddy did. I've seen some pictures of him and I would say, yeah I do. I'm 5' 6" tall, 170 pounds, light-skinned. Some people have said I looked like Juvenile. I wear glasses 'cause my eyes are bad. Without them on everything is blurry, therefore it's a must I have them unless I have contacts in. I don't know if my dad ever wore them or not and I never have asked anyone. All the pictures I've seen of him had no glasses on, though.

I can remember vaguely when I was around three or four years old, I would ride with my momma to take my daddy to work at like four or five in the mornin'. I've always woke up early, ever since I been a kid.

I still remember one time my momma and daddy were getting into it. Even though that was over twenty years—a long time ago—I still remember it. That's why it's important that me and Nelle do not do any fighting or arguing in front of the kids because they will definitely remember.

It's easy to get in the mind frame that it doesn't matter, because they are so young but that's a bad attitude to have. I want to be a role model to my kids, even though so far I've been a bad example. I smoked weed all day in front of them, I sold drugs in front of them, and drunk in front of them so long that it became as if it was nothing. I was playing with my daughter last time I was out and accidently burnt her on the finger with the blunt of popcorn weed I was smokin' on.

I've only been to one birthday party of my kids. It was a great one, though. I remember I cried, too. I cried tears of happiness and joy. It's a great feeling to be able to throw your kids a birthday party, especially for the first time. This summer when their birthdays come around, I'm gone give them another party. I'm excited about it, too.

***

"What up, Nelle?" I said as I came out of Pop-N-Go. "What you got goin' on?"

"Nothin'," she said, lookin all guilty of somethin'.

"Where's the kids at?" I say.

"They over at my momma's."

I shake my head. I just seen this dude name Beast Mode in the store. I was locked up at John Lilley Correctional Center in Boley with him. When he saw me in the store it was like he was in shock. I paid him no attention though, just paid for my gas and headed out the store.

I could tell that my wife was drunk and had been prolly takin' some bars or somethin' by the way her speech was slurred. She was tellin' me that she loved me and missed me a lot.

I just looked at her like, *yeah whateva*. I think her and this dude Beast Mode are messin' 'round 'cause Beast Mode's real name is Bryan Bucker and when I was in prison and I would look on Facebook, one time I went to her friend list to see who all she had on there because she was steady sayin' somethin' 'bout people I had on my friend list. I seen the name Bryan Bucker, but it did not have a picture of him. I asked her who that was and she said it was her classmate so I just left it alone although my suspicion was high in the sky.

I knew that Beast Mode was a scandalous-ass nigga. He was a dawg, too. He was from OKC from 7-7 IFG. He was about 6' 3" 230 pounds. He had muscles that bulged out of his shirt. I didn't trust him as far as I could see 'em cause I seen how he was in the pen. He was always tryna get over on the next man. Therefore, I didn't mess wit' em like that, besides what *up o*r a head nod.

He came out the store looking in the direction that me and my wife were. He walked to the side of the building as if he was about to walk off and then I guess he said forget it and went to the passenger-side of my wife's car and got in.

"Nelle, is this the nigga you been messin' wit'?" I angrily spoke.

"Yeah," she replied.

"Let's ride out," Beast Mode said to Nelle.

"You scandalous bitch-ass nigga," I said.

He got out the car, smilin'. I pulled out this all chrome .380 revolver that has six rounds loaded and pointed it directly over the top of the car at his face. He started coming around to where I was at.

"Charles, don't do it. Don't do it," Nelle was screamin'. "Y'all just stop, both y'all. Please!"

Pop... pop... pop...

I shot three rounds to his chest. As he grabbed his chest and stumbled back, I let loose the other three rounds.

"Ol' pussy ass nigga," I said as he lay on the ground shiverin' and shakin'. The white t-shirt he had on was bloody red, literaly, from the blood which was coming from his chest.

As I woke up from the dream, I had a severe headache and my heart was palpitating.

Chapter Six

"Count time! Count time! Count time!" this bald-headed super fat Humpty Dumpty lookin' C.O. was screamin' early in the morning which woke me up.

Stupid muthafucka, I thought. I was already pissed off from the dream I just had. Now my mind is wandering non-stop. I wonder if this dream is only soulish or is God tryna tell me somethin'. I believe that God speaks to us through dreams so whenever I have one I usually tend to ask myself this question. What is this dream telling me?

Today's a new day. It's the 15th of January which is Martin Luther King's real birthday. Also, it's my brother-in-law Fedro's birthday.

Thank you Father God for another day. Another day that was not promised to me. In the name of Jesus. . .

I've made it a habit to say that prayer every mornin' that I wake up. Every now and again I let it slip by but nine times out of ten I say it first thing in the morning. On the days I don't say it first thing, then I will at least say it before the day is over.

I picked up my daily devotional and read what it said:

> *When Your words came, I ate them;*
>
> *They were my joy and my heart's delight,*
>
> *for I bear your Name, O Lord God Almighty.*
>
> *Jeremiah 15:16*

Hmmm... I say, thinkin' how real that is. The words from the bible definitely give me joy and my heart delight. I finally come to truly, truly realize that only with Him can I make it. I realize that my flesh is weak and apart from Him the good I want to do, I can't do it. The wrong that I do, but try to stop, I cannot stop. I make promises that I mean to keep but I break them. One thang fa' sho about God is He can't lie so He is a promise keeper.

"I'm still tired," I say while yawning. I stand up, stretch, then grab my toothbrush and put some toothpaste on it. I grab my face cloth as well. I'm brushing my teeth while heading to the restroom to get fixed up. All the same time, I'm rappin' "Cross Life" by *Cross Life* in my head:

*Now I live a Cross Life, No longer
a Ruff Life
Use ta be a robber, I would run up
in yo' crib
Use ta be a drug dealer, getting it
how I live
Use to be a gangbanger and I was
a gun slanger*

*Now I live a Cross Life, AKA a
Boss Life
Cross Life, Boss Life, such a
wonderful life...*

* * *

Tryna do right for *me* sometimes seems is only a waste of time. I mean, I know it's not, but my feelings can sho nuff tag along with that idea. Every time I've gotten out of lockup I go back to drugs and alcohol. And when Ruff Dawg get messed up, I get wasted like the white boys. I'm not much of a club-goer but I do love to kick it. With me, I can kick it at the house or wherever I'm at. I make the party, the parties don't make me.

Besides that I know that the clubs are usually filled with demons and are infested in sin. I mean, let's be real.

If I'm going clubbin' every week or whatever, and I'm getting G'd up lookin' fresh ta death and on top, I'm a married man, but Ima very handsome young man then the ladies gone be on me. I might do good a hundred times or maybe one thousand, but one of those times Satan gone catch me vulnerable.

We all know the sayin', "If you hang around the barbershop too long, you gone get ya hair cut." That's real talk and I like to use that illustration in all parts of my life.

I'm different from most people I know because my thinkin' be off the wall. I am usually by myself because I don't become too close to many people and it's crazy too, cause mostly everybody love them some Ruff Dawg. If they say they don't, it's cause they hatin' and full of jealousy and envy. It's all good, though, cause they hated Jesus without cause, too. No matter what, I'm gone stay prayed up and not lose my focus right now or when I get out this time.

* * *

The last time I got out in 2011 I had lost my focus because of the amount of alcohol I started drinking and the Xanax bars I was poppin' and the weed in which I smoked like cigarettes. I quit smoking cigarettes in 2010 when I was in over there at Jackie Brannon Correctional Center in McAlester, Oklahoma.

I was working a full time job so that I could take care of my court fines, restitution and child support. On top of that, I had bills that needed to be paid and off the top, I had to provide for my family.

I went to the drug game to make extra money. I got in touch with some old clientele from the last time I was out and got it on with a quarter of dope. I flipped that a few times while stacking money up by the hunerds. I then bought a QP of weed from my potna, Johnny Papah, who stayed in Tulsa, but always came down to Muskogee to get off.

Johnny Papah was definitely about his papah. Every time you see him he is Archer's Cleaners clean, from the shirt all the way down. He wore a big gold rope around his neck with a gold dollar sign in which had diamonds all through it.

He is a lady's man, a chick magnet, but he did not love just one lady—he loved them all.

"I can't choose only one, when there's so many and I love each and every one of em," he would say all the time. His mouthpiece was cold too and he would talk salt outta its flavor.

He stood about my same height. He kept a taper fade and his wave game was vicious. He about the same skin tone lightness as me, too. Some people say we look like brothers.

I cop'd from him for about four months straight. I was buying two pounds each time I cop'd from him before I started dealing with another connect. I wasn't makin' any major money but I was steady stackin' money and did not have to ask no one for nothin'.

If I wanted to take my wife out to eat then I could do it. If we wanted to go trick off a hunerd or two at the casino, then we could do it. I ain't wit all that losin' big money to the casino no more because in 2006 I hit for 3600 dollars and gave it all back like an idiot.

I believe that Johnny Papah got knocked by the one times. His cell number kept goin' straight to the voicemail for about three days then the last couple times I tried, it made that noise then said, "we're sorry, the number you have dialed has been temporarily disconnected or is no longer in service."

I never tried calling again after that.

I bought me a truck so that I could finally have my own transportation. It's a hassle not having your own vehicle so I've always tried to have my own.

As the money started coming in, that's when I got a lil' big headed and started being arrogant. I felt like no one could tell me what to do cause I'm grown and making my own money. I'm paying bills and didn't feel the need to listen to what others were sayin' to me when they had specks of sin in their own lives.

The truth is, I should've listened because I believe that God speaks to me through other individuals. There is warning before destruction and I was warned and warned and warned. I thank God for His mercy and grace upon my life because I wouldn't be here if it wasn't for His mercy and grace.

I had three wrecks the last time I was out due to my drug and alcohol abuse. The last one was the one that I'm in for right now which is D.U.I.—causing great bodily injury.

I truly did not mean to hurt this guy and I sent my condolences to him and his family.

It was Martin Luther King Day, January 16th, 2012. I just picked up my son from the parade from my wife cause she was takin' my daughter to get her hair done. While I was picking my son up, I got a call from this girl I'd been talkin' to named Charmin who must have been passing through and seen me. She told me she wanted me to come over and chill fo' a minute so I said, *Okay, bet.* Besides, I wasn't doing much and no lie about it, Charmin was sexy. She stood 5' 4" tall with dark black hair that went down to the shoulder blades on her back. She was yellow-bone with green eyes and long eyelashes. Her smile was like the rising of the sun. When I first seen her it was hard not to keep my eyes locked on her.

I dropped my son over my other sister house and started heading over Charmin's. Well, I never made it over Charmin's cause on the way I accidentally hit a man on a motorcycle. Thank God he didn't die because manslaughter time is 85%. He did lose a leg though.

At times the whole scene replays in my mind. I wonder, was it really my fault or his fault? I wonder, could it have been avoided or what I could have done different in that situation. By the time I seen him it was too late. I tried to turn out the way but still hit him, then hit the pole in the middle part of HWY 69 and Military Boulevard.

I was in shock and not tryna be locked up in jail for nothing like that so I fled the scene as quick as possible. A Good Samaritan followed me to my sister's house on 18th Street and he must have been on the phone with the police at the same damn time. Within sixty seconds of me being in the house, the police had it surrounded.

I took the weed out my pocket as well as I took my jewelry off. Looking out the windows I then seen police in the front and back of the house where my truck was parked. Dogs barking, police beatin' on the back and front doors.

* * *

"Nelle, I'm goin' through some emotional, mental issues right now," I say.

"I don't know why," she replied.

"You already know, Nelle."

"I don't know unless you tell me."

"Okay, well, I been thinkin' that you still talkin' to that dude Tom Gun that you were messin' with. I don't want my son going to football practice with Tom Gun either when you and him had been messin' round."

"I don't know why you worried about him. Ain't nobody worried about him. Now, you need to be worried bout if I'm talkin' to someone *else*," she snapped. "Besides, he ain't coachin' football practice right now so it don't matter."

"Still, I don't want my son going to it whenever that was someone you had a lil' fling thing with. I mean, put yourself in my shoes," I said.

"It's nothin', it's only business," she snapped again. "I ain't got time for this shit right now. Call me back, later."

"Well, when do you ever have time to talk to me about what's goin' on in my life or what's bothering me? I come to you as a friend and I can't even get you to be my friend, so you know what—*Fuck you, bitch.*"

And I hung up the phone.

Chapter Seven

"Man, bro. I ended up cussin' my wife out on the phone. You know how you don't mean to do somethin' but it just comes out? I mean, homie, I be tryna talk to her about what's goin' on with me but she gets angry and acts like what I'm talkin' 'bout is nothin'. I'm really tired of messin' round wit this crazy woman. I love her but it's like I am not getting love back. It's gotta be them drugs she be on that got her always with an attitude. It's like she lost all respect fo' me. She is disrespectful towards me, even though not by callin' me names. She is disrespectful by bein' rude, bein' mean and not givin' me any support. I ask her questions, she won't eva answer me and it's to the point where I'm wasting my time with Nelle. I'm allowing her to control my emotioins and pull my strings like a puppet, which brings me outta character so I believe I have got to tell her it's over. I want this to work but there's no way to fit a square into a circle."

"Ruff, homie, Ima tell you this cause I love you dawg and I know that you a good nigga. I'm not saying to not be with her cause she yo' wife and I don't know her but maybe you can just back up from her cause I can see that she been havin' you down lately and havin' you on an emotional roller coaster. Both y'all need communication, understanding, and some kind of compromise. But #1 priority homie is y'all gotta—I repeat—y'all gotta—and I can't stress this enough—that y'all gotta keep God first and in the center of y'all relationship. Both y'all gotta be on that some page or mission homie, unless you already knowin' that shit ain't gone work."

"That's real talk T," I said. "Appreciate you lettin' me chop it up with you big dawg. You know I'm gone first thing in the mornin'. It's been three years exactly and I'm ready to ride out."

"Fa' sho, Fa' sho, Ruff. You knowin' we gone stay locked in."

"Already," I said

* * *

Today is the day and it's a great day because I'm up outta this joint. January 16th, 2015 is finally here. I got all my stuff boxed up that I'm gone take with me. Stuff like my bible, my poem book, about three lyric books, two books by Robert Greene: *Art of Seduction* and *48 Laws of Power*. Also, one other book by James Allen called *The Mind is a Master*. I gave my TV and a pair of Flight 9 Jordans to T to help him out because I knew him from the world.

Yesterday, my unit manager told me that he would take me to Muskogee instead of driving me to the bus station in Oklahoma City. While waiting, I chop it up with some potnas that I've met in here. I met some real cool people here and hope the best for them all.

"Ruffin? Are you ready?" Mr. Johns said.

"I been ready. Is it that time to leave?"

"Yep. Take your box of belongings to the gatehouse and I will be there in five minutes."

"Okay," I said. I head to property, grab my box and make my way to the gatehouse with an ear to ear smile on my face.

"It's on, Ruff Dawg!" a lotta the inmates say as I'm on my way to the gatehouse. I already got my potnas into in which I'm keepin' touch so I'm just ready to go.

"C'mon Ruffin. Let's go," my unit manager Mr. Johns said. "The black four-door truck right there by the yellow car is the one we will be driving in." He points his keychain thang at the truck to unlock the doors. I open the door and to my surprise it is very nice inside.

"I love this truck, Mr. Johns. It's just right for me. I'm gone get me one just like this. What year is it?" I asked.

"It's a 2014 Silverado. I'm glad you like it, Ruffin, and I'm here to tell you if this is something you want then you can get it. I believe that."

* * *

It feels good to be free now. No chains are on me and I'm headed back to my hometown. It's 9:30 AM and I still got all day when I get there. I really don't know what I'm gone do honestly. None of my people know that today is the exact day I'm coming home, either. They all know soon, though. By 11 AM I will be in Muskogee. It only takes about an hour and 15 minutes to get there from Boley prison.

Mr. Johns is over there driving fast so I know he is tryna hurry and get me home so he can get back to the prison. The radio station is on some Country station. I ain't trippin' though, cause I've actually started to like country. The song on right now is Scott Dylan, *Makin' This Boy Go Crazy*. I like this song. I use to hear it a lot on Channel 12, ZUUS TV.

We pass a sign that says *Welcome to McAlester* so I know we are getting closer to the town. Now, I'm thinkin' bout getting me a dime sack of weed and a bottle of Hennessey and celebrating my release. I know I don't need to, but shoot, after bein' locked up this three years I'm ready to kick back and have some fun.

I ain't been out with my momma since 2008 when we both got locked up. I got out in January 2011, but came back in January 2012. Momma got out in May 2014 but she ain't been able to come see me because she's been on ankle monitor. She got off last month in December but the visitation forms take so long to get approved that she still had not got approved. I wasn't trippin' though, 'cause I knew I was 'bout to get out. Momma has been my big support and without her I truly don't know what I would do. From the beginning when I first started doing time at fifteen, momma has always been there.

I thank God for my momma and that's where I'm gone be staying for a while until I get myself situated. She don't know I'm pulling up today so she gone be surprised.

My thoughts are everywhere right now. Thinking bout my kids Charles and Charliah; thinkin' bout my wife Nelle and how thangs gone be with us.

It's so much goin' through my mind that it's kinda depressing but I'm so happy to be released from prison that it is what it is. I ask that God's will be done in my life and I trust Him to work out all things in Jesus' name.

"Ruffin," Mr. Johns broke the silence between us.

"Sir."

"I was sittin' here thinkin' and I done took many inmates home from prison when they made parole or discharged. Many of them I see get back into trouble and some even get killed and it saddens my heart, tremendously. I want you to know that I believe in you. I noticed the way you carried yourself on the yard and you were always respectful and I never heard anything bad about you from inmates or staff. That's a compliment too, because for your age, you conduct yourself very good. What I'm basically tryna say is your destiny lies in your hands. You got a new start from this day forward. You can choose to stay outta the game or you can choose to go back into it but whatever you choose to do, know that you have a choice. All I'm sayin' is to choose the right choice instead of the wrong choice, because we both know that there is consequences in the game and the game ain't nothin' but a shame. I'm not tellin' you nothin' you don't know already, or that no one else prolly hasn't told you many of times. I don't mean to sound like a broken record, but I just want you to know that I care about whether you succeed or fail in life. I've never done this before, but I feel led to leave you my phone number, just in case there is any way I can help you in the future, you will have my info and I give you my word that as long as the Lord wills I will do my best."

"Thanks, Mr. Johns," I said, lookin' him directly in his eyes. I could tell that he was dead serious by the tears that had formed in his eyes.

Honk...Honk...

The car behind Mr. Johns blew letting him know to go as the light had turned green on HWY 69 as we were entering Muskogee. The car containing a group of young thugs flipped us off and was throwing up gang signs to us as they sped off.

"Crazy stuff in the city of the Gee," I said. "That's why I'm gone get away from here, soon. Anyway, Mr. Johns, I appreciate those kind words and I will keep yo number and if I need you I will definitely holler."

"A man's word is a man's self-love. A man that keeps his word loves himself. And I do love myself," Mr. Johns said with a smile.

All I could do was nod my head up and down while saying, "Yeah, you right about that one. Keep going up this way on HWY 69 until you reach Okmulgee Street and turn right. We 'bout five minutes from my momma's house where I will have you drop me off. I'm a little nervous," I said. "Not knowing what to expect, but one thing I know is that God got my back so I'm gone be alright. I claim that in the name of Jesus."

"In the name of Jesus," Mr. Johns replied. "I am glad I got to talk to you and be able to bring you here because I enjoyed this conversation."

"Thank you. I'm glad you did."

* * *

Mr. Johns was alright, I guess. I really didn't talk to him much in the penn, though. Most the time, I just went to my case manager, Mr. Penn. I did have an altercation with him once, though. He came on the unit and was trippin' taking everybody's stuff if you didn't have a property sheet on it. In other words, if it's from the yard, then he was takin' it.

I tried to be slick and used my coat and put my TV in there and gave it to this guy named Sam to take it to the front where he had already checked. The dude got busted because he just stood there looking stupid once he got to the dayroom.

Mr. Johns booked em, and put the jacket and the TV in the basket.

I'm like, *aint this a bitch?*

I tried to get it back after he left out but he was not going for it, which had me mad but I blew it off cause I did it to myself to keep it a hundred.

Besides that though, me and Mr. Johns didn't have a problem.

Chapter Eight

"Alright, Mr. Johns. I thank you for everything," I said as he pulled up to my mom's house. I started to get out of his truck when he said, "Hold up, Ruffin. Don't forget my phone number."

"Thanks, I'm glad you reminded me," I said. Mr. Johns grabbed a piece of paper and gave me his information. "Have a safe trip back," I said. I grabbed my box out of the backseat of the truck and headed to the front door.

Right before I got to knock on the door, it opened. "Hey, Momma," I said as she kissed me and embraced me in her arms as tight as she could.

"I love you, Charles. Bring ya stuff in. Why you didn't tell nobody you was getting out? Did you not know it?"

"I was wanting to surprise everyone so don't tell nobody. I ain't told Nelle either, so I'm just gone sneak up on her unexpected later on. For right now I needa get in the shower and get refreshened up. I got a lot to take care of today."

"Okay! Well, after you get dressed, do you want to go grab something to eat?"

"I sure do, Momma."

Well, well, well, I say to myself. I'm fresh released from lockup and this go round I'm not tryna ever go again. I never actually try anyway, but seem to end up there, therefore, I gotta stick to the script and keep God number one. I can't be what people call a bible thumper, one who gets close to God while locked up and then once released, forget all about Him.

"Momma, how does Smoke House Bob's sound?"

"If that's what you want, then let's go and we can get some cause you know I don't mind."

We go to Smoke House Bob's and knock off some BBQ ribs, fried fish, and okra while sittin', choppin' it up about what's been happenin' lately.

"I'm glad you out Charles and want you to stay out this time cause Momma ain't goin' back. I loves my freedom."

"I won't, Momma," I said. I couldn't help myself but to drift off in wonderland, thinkin' about how thing's would be with me and Nelle. Am I gone try to make it work or am I just gone be a bachelor full-time. Apart of me says *forget Nelle* since she done me dirty, but on the other hand I truly do love her and want to be with her as a family.

Ring. . . Ring. . .

My Momma's phone starts to ring which brought me back to the present. "Who that Momma?"

"This Nicole. She wants to talk to you."

"What up sis? Chillin'…sittin' here eatin' with Momma….bout to be leaving now. What up with you?"

"I just got off work. I didn't know you were getting out today."

"Yeah, I know. I didn't tell anybody I was just using the element of surprise."

"Have you seen yo' kids yet?"

"Nawll, I ain't really seen anybody yet. It's actually the first time I done moved around since I been in town and ain't called nobody, either."

"Well, I will talk to you later and I love you."

"Love you, too."

"Tell Momma I'll talk to her later."

"Okay."

"Nicole said she will talk to you later, Momma."

"Momma, I need to go to the court house and check in today. I got three days, but the faster I get it done I won't have to worry about it for a while."

"Okay, I'm gone take you now," Momma said.

Muskogee looks different now. A few new restaurants, motels, and houses built. The police have not changed cause every other corner we turn we see one. The cops stay hot in the Gee.

"Let me off right here, Momma and I will run in this court house right quick. I will try not to be long. As I enter into the double glass doors I'm already feeling exhaustion. The memory of comin' in and out of this court house not knowing if I will be getting locked up or not. You never know what type of stuff these people will pull.

On the 2nd floor I enter into the court clerk office. An older black woman in her fifties asks, "How may I help you?"

"Ma'am, I just got outta prison today and was told to be up here."

"Do you have your release papers?"

"Yes I do. Sorry about them being folded up."

"It's no problem, come follow me to the back and we will arrange your payments. It looks like you have around five thousand dollars to pay in restitution and eighteen thousand in court fines. We usually arrange them at $100 a month but I will set yours at fifty a month. You will have until next month on the 15th of February to pay. If you do not have any questions, then I am done with this procedure."

"Okay, thanks, and have a good day," I said as I rise up and leave out her office and leave the court clerk room.

Now I need to go to the 4th floor so I enter the elevator and press 4. I hate talkin' to these probation people but I gotta do what I gotta do. *Who could be my PO?* I wonder. As I go into the probation and parole office I see Mr. Cheeks which is a straight up dickhead. He always acts like he knows me, but he don't know me like that. He has never been my PO either, but it's only two probation officers here at the court house and the last time I had Mrs. Readdy so I always would see him. When I had to take UAs, he was the one who would watch me as I piss in the cup.

"Hello, my name is Charles Ruffin and today I got released from prison so I am trying to figure out who is my probation officer."

"Mr. Ruffin, are you gone stay out this time?" Mr. Cheeks said with a smug on his face.

"Of course," I said while lookin' at him with a mug. I wanted to say, *Fuck you, pussy muthafucka,* but I knew that would only make things worse.

"Fill out that paper right there on the clipboard and then I will take your picture."

"Okay," I said. "Mr. Cheeks, what happened to Mrs. Readdy?"

"Oh, she got another job so she left."

"Okay, just wonderin'."

The paper I'm filling out reminds me of all the many times I use to come in and fill it out in the past. My name, my address, phone number, job, any police contact, vehicle description, etc. It didn't take long to fill it out and hand it back to him.

"My Momma is waiting on me so I'm tryna hurry up as quick as possible."

"Alrighty then. I will be your probation officer this go round. Keep your nose clean and you won't have any problems. Let's take your picture and I will let you get up outta here until next month."

Mr. Cheeks gives me a mugshot to the front, one facing to the left, and one facing to the right.

"Here's your next appointment; 9 AM on February 20th. I will see you later."

I hurry up and get outta there and back to the elevator to get out this court house. It's now 3:30 PM and now I'm thinkin' 'bout gettin' blowed back since I done seen my PO. As I exit the court house I see my Momma's black Kia Optima parked in the bank parking lot across from the court house. I jog across the street before the cars can pass and get back into my Momma's car.

"People been callin', wantin' to talk to you. I told 'em you was in the court house. You know Nicole done told everybody you was out."

"I already knew she was cause Nicole can't keep her mouth shut. I don't blame her though. It's all good. Momma, will you take me by Nelle's so I can see the kids. I know they will be happy to see me."

"Okay, I will Charles, but don't go over there trippin' with that girl."

"I ain't gone be trippin' wit her, Momma."

"Yeah, I know you," Momma said while poochin' out her lips.

It's been nine months since I've seen my kids or Nelle. Once she jumped out the car, she has not came to see me since I knew she did not want to look me in the face knowin' how dirty she did me. Instill she should have brought the kids to see me. She said she was when she got the money but she ain't been concerned about visiting me. She rather spend her money on Xanax pills and liquor. Not to mention poppin' her coochy in the club on some random ass nigga that she thinks looks good.

As we pull up I see Nelle's red Maxima on 22" rims with tinted windows parked in the driveway. My heart rate is pounding like a drum as I exit the vehicle and approach the front porch.

I say a small prayer. *God please help me to control myself in here, in Jesus' name.* I ring the doorbell once...twice...

"Who is it?" I hear Nelle's voice screamin'. "Oh! It's y'all daddy. Charles, Charliah. Y'all daddy!"

Nelle opens the door lookin' sexy in a purple silk robe. I can tell that she has no bra on, so... I can't help but think she ain't got no panties on, either. Her chocolate skin tone lookin' like a Milky Way got me ready to take a bite. Neither one of us say a word to one another. I wanted to say *let me hit that coochie like you been lettin' everybody else*, but I decided that would be too disrespectful.

"Daddy! Daddy!" My kids jump into my arms as I enter inside the house.

"I love y'all and miss y'all. Do y'all miss y'all Daddy?"

"Yeah! We wanna go with you. Can we, Daddy? Please! Please!"

"Right now, Daddy is living with Big Momma so maybe Saturday y'all can come stay with me."

"Daddy, why ain't you stayin' wit us," my daughter asked.

"Yeah, Daddy. We want you to stay here with us and Momma," my son added.

"Well, I'm not sure about all that right now kids. It's a lot going on with me and Momma that y'all would not understand right now. I had to come by to see y'all and I will be hollerin' at y'all again tomorrow. I love y'all and y'all be good."

"I love you too, Daddy," both my kids said as I turned around and headed out the door.

"Dang. You act like you couldn't say nothin' to me, Charles. I see how you is," Nelle said, hanging out the door as I opened my Momma's car to get inside.

I looked back at her and said nothin'. I get in the car and see that my Momma is on the phone. She takes off going faster than usual so I did not say nothin', just sat there wondering what has happened. She is saying nothing on the phone, just listening. Now I'm concerned as she almost hit a man who was walking across the street.

"Momma, what's going on? What's going on, Momma?" I repeated myself.

"Momma's house done burned down and I'm tryna get over there to make sure they are alright."

If it ain't one thing it's another I said to myself. It's Friday, I'm fresh up outta lockup and already, family problems going on.

As we pull up I see my grandma Precious and my Uncle Marty standing. My grandma was talking to the police. The firemen were finishing extinguishing the house and putting all their hoses up. I was so happy to see my grandma that I ran up to her and gave her a big hug and kiss. It's been three years since I've seen grandma and she is getting up there in age. She's eight-four years old now. She's still energetic, though. You will catch her outside cleaning and raking the dirt in the front yard or the backyard.

"What up Unc?" I shake his hand with my right hand, and with my left I give him a hug. "I'm glad to see you Unc. Hate I had to see y'all like this but I'm thankful that y'all got up out the house. God is good."

Uncle Marty is an OG from Lime Hood Piru and has respect in Muskogee from Bloods and Crips alike. He got out the penn from doing ten flat and his mind was thrown off. I heard that some Indians tried to kill him in there over some beef that they had going on and it messed him up.

When I was young, I actually wanted to be like Uncle Marty, though I never told him. I remember when I was six years old, maybe seven, I seen him shoot a man who was from the other side. Ol' dude came up trippin' with him with his crew and Unc was not tryna be trippin' because he was at his niece T.P.'s birthday party, which is my sister. One of the dudes stole on him and the fight took place but when another one tried to run up Unc took out the Chrome .380 from his waistband.

Now everyone is screaming, "He *gotta gun, he gotta gun!*" It was too late for one of them who slipped and fell and Unc gave him two shots to the chest and one in the stomach. Afterwards he ran off from the apartment complex that we were living in at the time in Muskogee called Sugar Tree.

Chapter Nine

By this time the whole family and town knows that Ruff Dawg is back on the streets. I was trying to keep it hush but it's hard in the City of the Gee. In Muskogee everybody always in yo' business and always gossipin'.

I don't wanna go back to the same stuff but today I'm fresh released *so forget it* I tell myself. I'm gone kick it today.

All my family and friends are gathered here over my Momma's greeting me and showin' me mad love by giving me daps and hugs. They givin' me money so I will have some pocket change.

"Roll up," Monkey says as she hugs me tightly and tells me how much she misses me and been ready for me to touch turf. "I been tellin' everybody bout you and you know the bitches been waitin' on you. I got a few lined up right now."

"Fa' sho, FAM," I say as she throws some purple kush at me that drops and hits the floor. I pick it up and say, "You already got a stick!"

Monkey is one of my favorite cousins. She is my first cousin and we've been close forever but especially since I was about fourteen years old when we moved back to Muskogee from Coweta, Oklahoma. Monkey is light-skinned about the same complexion as me. She's a pretty young lady who reminded me of Queen Latifah. Monkey has an attitude and personality out of this world, though. On top, she has been known to be a permissive female. But she my cousin and I love her no matter what.

"This smell fire, Monkey! Where you get this from?" I say as I breakdown the sticky buds. I use my thumbnail to split the White Owl Swisher Sweet open to fill it up.

"I'm glad you finally back out, FAM. You know it's still family first.

"No doubt," I say. "As a matter of fact, I wrote a song called *Still Family First*. I'm 'bout to blow up in this music industry this go round, fam."

"Fasho and you can do it Charles. I believe in you cause you got talent."

"Appreciate that family. I'm glad to hear that you believe in me. Where the flame at so I can light this blunt."

"Here. Where is Nelle at? I'm surprised she ain't over here right now. Is y'all still together?"

"I don't know about her honestly. We suppose to be workin' out our marriage but she lies so much that I really don't trust her no more and since she done left me for her other guy it just ain't the same no more."

"Yeah, I understand that," Monkey said. I saw her with Quan yesterday at the store. What was Quan doin' drivin' her car?"

"Ain't no tellin'. That's prolly some Nigga she messin' wit', too. That's why I can't trust her. She ain't gone admit it either so that's why I'm highly thinkin' bout sayin' fuck her. Besides, that marriage bed is so defiled that I don't want to be in it no more."

"That's real. Well, Charles, I want the best for you cause you my family; you my day one."

"This some fire weed you got," I say as I pass it to Monkey distracting her from talkin' bout Nelle, whom I didn't wanna talk about. "Do you got some bars?"

"I got prolly five. Here, Ima give you two of 'em."

"Bet dat. Ima get tow back today. I'm tryna hit da club tonight, too. Do you got some wheels?"

"You know I do! That black Chevy Caprice is mine down there by the stop sign."

"Oh, okay. I see you kinfolk. That's what up, cause Ima need you tonight to take me. It's only 8:15 PM now and I'm high than a mug cause I ain't even been blowin' back. Actually, I stopped cause I been tryna change, but you know how that goes."

"Believe me, I know Charles, but it be too damn hard out here goin' through all this bullshit from day to day."

"I know. That's why you gone have to give me the word on the street so I can know what's poppin down here in the Gee. I needah know who makin' noise round here so I can know what to look for."

"I got you, fa' sho. I'm down with you to the fullest extent. No doubt."

"Already," I say as I finish puffin' on the last puff of the now doobie then I throw it on the ground.

"What's up, Charles? Charles Ruffin!" I hear someone say but couldn't see who it was then I see my sister T.P. and her husband Dex and kids approachin' me with big smiles upon their faces. They all gave me hugs and tell me how they are glad that I'm out.

"Where ya wife and kids at?"

"I don't know," I say. "I saw them earlier but that's it. I don't know if I'm messin' wit' her cause she on some other shit."

"Boy, you know you love that girl," T.P. said.

"I know I love her, but that doesn't mean I'm a dummy. I'm tryna move forward and messin' with her could lead me backwards. It's gone be different without being with her no more after ten years but, hey, people grow apart. Honestly, T.P. I don't hate her but I actually feel hate in my heart towards her for how she went about handling the situation. Really, I don't even give a fuck no moe," I said feeling myself getting pissed just talkin' bout her.

"What up, Bro?" J3 said.

"Bro, I just been chillin' and tryna get my thoughts together," I say as I give J3 a hug.

J3 was a lady's man. He's my older brother by a year. Actually, 363 days cause for 2 days we are both the same age. J3 is about 5'11" tall with brown skin. Some say we look alike except he's darker. J3 never got into the gangs like I did but he did start selling drugs for a little while and was getting his gwap until one time he got setup and got popped. He quit sellin' crack cocaine and went to only marijuana which he provided the town of Muskogee for a while with some light-tight Reggie and loud packs. Bro kept them bricks by the duffel bag but once again he was setup and got busted in his east side of Tulsa home.

"Bro, I'm thinkin' 'bout taking you up on your offer and moving with you to Tulsa," I said.

"You need to, man. I'm tryna tell you 'cause if you stay down here in Muskogee you mess around and get back into trouble. That's why I got away from here. Ain't nothin' in Muskogee."

"That's real talk, bro. So I'm glad that you down with it so I can move around. By the way, bro, we heading to the club tonight to kick it if you tryna come with us."

"Alright, I'm down. We might as well all go just to kick it since today you out."

"Bet dat. We gone be ridin' out 'bout eleven tonight to go to the club, Reflections.

Chapter Ten

Before I got locked up I bought lots of clothes and shoes that I never got to wear so I am fitted from head to the feet as we step up into Reflections. I'm feelin' myself to the max right now off the two bars that I popped and the blunt of purp that I smoked a little earlier. The club is jumpin' tonight. I'm getting mad love from all the fellas and the ladies who I knew before I got locked up.

"What up Ruff Dawg?" 2 Sweet said as he approached me with 2 bad yellow-bones on his side. They looked like twins 'cause they both were thicky thicky thick with long hair. One had green eyes and the other had brown eyes.

"I'm just chillin', bro. Fresh outa lockup and tryna have a good time. I see you havin' a lovely time with these lovely ladies you with.

"Aww, man, you know how I do it. I try to keep somethin' nice. I ain't trippin' like that though; if you want you can have one of 'em. What's yo' pick?"

"It's a hard pick, really, because I want both of 'em but right now I'm just peepin' out the scene. If they are around later, I'm prolly gone needah scoop one up though. By the way, ladies, what's y'all name?"

"Shonda," the one on the left said as she blushed and the one on the right said, "My name is Ms. Beautiful and later on you'll have a beautiful time wit' me."

"Alright now Beautiful, I'll see what you talkin' 'bout then cause it sounds like you offerin'."

"I damn sho' am cause as fine as you is, I'm knowin' you got some bomb dick and you fresh out. I'm tryna get some of that."

I chuckle then turn my attention back to 2 Sweet and let em know I will catch up with 'em.

It's some bad lil' broads up in here, I'm thinkin' to myself. A lot of new faces that I ain't seen in Muskogee when I was out last time.

"Come on, bro," J3 said. "Let's grab some drinks. It's time to celebrate."

"Alright. Bet, bro. You know I'm down. I was just checkin' out the scene up in here and hollerin' at a lotta peeps who glad to see me. Well, I know it's all fake cause when I was on lock, what'n nan one carin' about me or even thinkin' about me because when you out of sight you out of mind."

"What you tryna drank, Charles?"

"Whatever you drinkin', I'm drinkin'."

"Two cups of Hennessey and Hypnotic mix," bro said to the bartender who looked like Candy, this chick that I had hit back in the day when I was fifteen. She made the drinks and brought them back while starin' at me.

"Charles? Is that you?"

"Yeah, it's me. What's poppin' sexy thang?"

"Shoot, I thought that was you. It's been a while since we kicked it. Maybe we can get together one day and chill for old time's sake."

"It's on," I said as I turned and walked off. It's not that I didn't want to chill with her but I am not too concerned wit' the old chicks from the past cause they old news, besides, I heard Candy been getting ran through by them Summit niggas and those is some nasty ass niggas. Candy is sexy chocolate and fine as can be, don't get me wrong, but instill—I'm cool.

I turn my head towards the entrance and see what looks like my wife Nelle comin' in with her sisters and some niggas they with. One of the niggas put his arm around my wife as they head toward the bar. I seen she was just a laughin' and smilin' and havin' a good time so I figure this must be some nigga she talkin' to. I know she did not see me so I was gone sit and play the background but bein' me, I couldn't. My heart dropped to my nuts as I pushed back to the bar, boilin' hot.

"Nelle, what type of shit you on, you triflin' ass bitch. I caught yo' hoe ass this time. I knew you whatn't shit."

"Nigga, ain't nobody got time fo' yo' bullshit. Ain't nobody messin' wit' this nigga. He is just my friend. Why you assumin' shit and jumpin' to conclusions? If you wanted to know you should've just asked."

"Shut up stupid ass bitch, I ain't no dummy. Come correct when you talkin' to me."

"Hold up, homie. You ain't gotta be dissin' her like that," the nigga said who was with her.

"Hey nigga. Fuck you, bitch ass nigga. This my muthafuckin' wife, so if you gotta problem we can handle up, but this ain't got shit to do with you. I ain't no hater. As a matter fact, you can have the hoe. Have fun Nelle, you stupid ass bitch."

* * *

"Dang, fam," Monkey said. "You went left on her."

"I know. I don't be tryin' to but she can get up under my skin real easy with that snake ass shit and then to stand there and lie in my face. Now she ain't got nothin' comin' with me. She wasn't expectin' me to be in the club tonight and her hoe ass got caught up. Now I know and see with my own eyes that she was still talkin' to other niggas, but steady tellin' me that she wasn't. She got me boilin' hot now. No lie. Let's go over there and sit back for a minute or two. You ain't got any more of the bomb?"

"You know I do."

Monkey dug in her bra and tossed me a stick and the weed and said, "twist up" as we sat across from each other at the table.

The lights are very dim in this club. It's about fifty people on the dance floor jiggin' to 2 Chains, *started from the trap now I rap, no matter where I'm at, I got crack...I got crin-ack, I got crin-ack...* Out of the corner of my eyes I seen Candy starin' over at me but I was tryin' to ignore her. She came from behind the bar to pick up a cup off the floor and bent over. I couldn't help but notice how thick she was. Her thighs looked like some ham hocks and the Apple Bottom jeans she had on with the red thong showin' immediately made my dick rise.

I lick my lips while my eyes are steady plugged on her. She looks back at me like, *yeah, nigga. This is what you are missing.*

No lie, I did wanna hit that at this moment after seeing that fat round ass that she knew how to make jiggle like Jell-O when she walked.

"Look at *this* bitch," I said as Nelle comes over to the table.

Nelle is lookin' sexy than ever, I have to be honest, but she's my wife and I ain't gone share no woman when it's so many. Nelle had on a pair of white skin-tight jeans that hugged her legs like they were painted on and I could see her fat ass pussy through the pants. She had on some black high heels and a silk black see-thru dress shirt with a white tube-top underneath that made her titties stick out somethin' crucial.

"What the fuck you want?" I said.

"Charles, why you doin' me like this? You know I love you. I told you I'm sorry for leaving you in there and I want to work on our marriage. When you came over earlier you act like you couldn't even say hi to me then you see my friend with me and you want to talk shit to me in this club. What's yo' problem?"

"For one, I'm not stupid, Nelle. You can call him your friend all you want but I don't believe. What is another nigga all on you for? Let me guess—because you drunk. Was you drunk last night when you had the nigga driving yo' car?"

"It was nothin' like that. You is trippin'."

"Well, bitch. I don't even care no more. Do *you* and Ima do *me*. Besides, when I was doin' time you forgot about me. I was in the penn and you forgot about me so now I'm on the streets, go ahead and forget about me."

"Please, Charles. Just—"

I cut her off. "Bitch! You drunk and on them pills and just talkin' so get gone. I ain't tryna hear it. Go and dick chase like you been doin' the three years I was gone. You had yo' time, now it's my time to shine. Here's the blunt, Monkey. Ima be right back. This liquor done ran through me."

As I get up to go to the restroom, which is next to the bar, Nelle tries to grab my hand. I push it down to the side. "Don't touch me."

I felt as all eyes were on me as I walked to the restroom. I bumped into a tall mix dude with dreadlocks as I entered. He looked at me wit' a look that said, lil *nigga, watch out!* His teeth were gold with diamonds on the top and the bottoms were all gold slugs. His thick gold rope chain had a crushed out dollar sign filled with diamonds. He had a watch that matched. His clothes were starched pressed and he looked like money so I could tell that he must have been a drug dealer, or some kinda figure in the game.

"My bad, homie," I said and pushed right by him. The 10x10 restroom smelled of urine from all the drunkards coming in, tryin' to aim in the urinal but pissing on the floor. "Let me hurry up out this muthafucka," I said.

I take my glasses off my face, cup some water in my hands and splash it on my face. I then grab some paper towels out the dispenser, dry my face, put back on my glasses and push out the door.

"It's the last song of the night," I hear the DJ screamin' over the loud speaker. "Grab ya shawty by the arm and bring her to the dance floor. Ima leave ya wit' a nice slow jam. *Suffocate* by J Holiday."

"Aww, shit. That's my song," Ms. Beautiful said as she locked eyes with me standing directly in front of her.

I don't know how we met up right here like this, because I damn sho' was not planning on actually makin' nothin' happen wit' Ms. Beautiful.

*I can't breathe when you talk to me, I can't breathe when ya touchin' me, I suffocate when you're away from me, so much love you take from me, I'm goin' outta my mind...*the song plays.

I nod my head at Ms. Beautiful as she grabs my arm as if she was my woman or somethin'. I did not resist, though. I went with the flow. Besides, Ms. Beautiful looks like Alicia Keys, accept thicker. It's somethin' I love about females with long hair.

Her juicy lips with lip glosss on 'em make me wanna kiss on 'em but I don't know her like that but instill, I'm horny than a muthafucka right now. She is walkin' me to the dance floor for this final song.

Fuck it, I say to myself and grab her fat round ass. She looks back and smiles, which only makes both my heads bigger. My dick rock hard and my ego an elephant.

Ms. Beautiful puts her arms around my neck as I put my arms around her waist. The dance floor is so packed that people are damn near touching one another. My dick pressed up against her pussy as I slide my hands down her backside and squeeze her ass cheeks into my dick. Her head now rested on my shoulder as we sway back in forth to the music.

I see J3 on Shonda and I couldn't help but smile. Bro shakes his head up and down like, *yeah nigga, I'm in there* and smiles back at me.

It feels real good to have my dick all over a woman for the first time in so long. I mean, besides the times Nelle would come visit me and I would put my dick all over her while the guards were not looking. I wanted to fuck her in that visitation room so many times, but she whatn't tryna be fuckin' in public. She did let me play with the pussy a few times, but she was stingy with that pussy with me. I know why now and that's because she was steady givin' the pussy to all them other niggas.

Stupid bitch, I say to myself.

"That's it for tonight. I hope you all have enjoyed your time here at Reflections. We will see ya next week, same time…" the DJ says.

"What you got goin' on now Ruff Dawg?" Ms. Beautiful said. "Or what is yo' real name so I can call you by that."

"I'm tryna ride out with you, sexy, cause I ain't got nothing going on beside tryna chill with you. And my name is Charles."

"Bro," I screamed as he turned his attention to me and nodded what up.

"Tell everybody Ima get back wit' 'em cause I'm goin' wit' homegirl right here for tonight."

"It's on bro," he said then I watched as he kept it pushin'. I figure he was about to knock ol' Shonda off.

Ain't no tellin' where 2 Sweet at either cause I ain't seen that nigga since earlier. Knowin' him, he prolly done knocked some other scallywags or somethin'.

Chapter Eleven

Beautiful immediately takes her clothes off as we enter into her apartment in Country Club. Her big titties are lookin' good. Her nipples are hard and I know that she is horny. She has no stomach and her bald pussy is lookin' fat and juicy. I stand in amazement as she locks the door.

"What you waitin' on nigga? Don't tell me you scared," Beautiful joked.

"I'm far from scared lil' mama, believe that," I say as I take my shirt off.

By this time she is on me unbucklin' my belt and pants button. My dick rock hard, she drops my pants and boxers and spits on the head of my dick then she licks it off with her tongue. She puts her mouth on the head of my dick and sucks on it like a lollypop as she uses her left hand to jack my dick off.

"Damn this feels good," I moan as she starts filling her mouth with all 6 inches of my dick. My hands on her head as she is slurpin' away and the sounds have got me thinkin' on when Nelle last sucked my dick before I got locked up. My legs begin to shake so I know I'm about to bust in her mouth so I hold her head even tighter as she deep-throats my dick like one of those porn stars you would see on Pornhub.com.

"Awww, yeah," I say as I bust off in her mouth, lookin' at her face as she continues suckin' all the juices out my dick.

Feelin' the tinglin' sensation, I start pushin' her head away. She looks up at me, lickin' her lips and makin' sure she swallows all my cum.

"You got some bomb juices," she said. "Nothin' like these niggas out here nowadays."

I kick my shoes off as well as my pants and boxers.

"Come beat my pussy up now," Beautiful says as I follow her down the hallway to her bedroom. She hops up on the bed and puts her legs behind her head. "Yeah, I know I'm flexible."

"Yeah, you is and I'm gone beat that pussy up just like you want, too." I stick my dick in her slowly while I have my hands on her ankles which are wrapped around her head.

"Damn!" she moans.

I give her a few slow strokes as she says *Faster, Faster!* So I put my entire dick inside her holding nothing back. My hips moving fast, I'm tryna kill her pussy as she moans and groans. The bed rockin' and the headboard is bouncin' against the wall.

"It's all yours, Charles. Beat this pussy up," Beautiful moans. Her hips thrusting just as fast as mine as we both are beginning to sweat. Her pussy is tight like vicegrips to my surprise. Her legs beginning to shiver and shake at the same time my breathing is increased and my strokes are now deep and slow instead of fast like a jack rabbit. I bust off in her as I feel her pussy walls tighten up tighter around my dick. We both climax at the same time.

"It's yo' turn," I say as I lay back on my back, dick still rock hard.

Beautiful immediately follows my lead and climbs on top of me. She grabs my dick and places it in her pussy hole as she begins grinding on my dick in a circular motion. She does that for about a minute or two before she leans in toward my chest and starts pussy poppin' on my dick. Her ass bouncin' all over me. I grab hold of her wide hips and hold on to them as she continues ridin' my dick faster and faster. Her moans growing louder and louder. Beautiful starts suckin' on my neck while thrusting her pussy forcefully on me. My ass muscles tight as she is riding my dick like a true cowgirl.

"You got some good pussy, girl. I might have to visit you again," I say as I nut all in her pussy. Both my hands now on her waist. Beautiful has her head back now, just slowly grinding on my dick as she gets off all on my dick. She rolls off of me as I get up.

"I hope you on birth control," I say. "Cause I done busted all up in yo' ass and I ain't tryna be getting you pregnant, fresh out."

"I got my tubes tied after I had my last lil' boy, Ben-Ben, cause I ain't tryna have no more, either. I got three already. Two boys and a girl is enough.

"Oh, okay. Well, I need to get cleaned up. Where's a towel or somethin'?"

"The bathroom is right across from my room and you will see the washcloths on the shelf and the soap," Beautiful said.

"Bet dat."

Ms. Beautiful had a clean bathroom which I was glad to see cause if a woman's bathroom is dirty, then ain't no tellin' what *else* is dirty. A little black clock radio sat on the shelf that read 5:45 AM. I wipe myself off and take a piss then go back in the front room and grab my clothes and put them on.

"Beautiful. Beautiful," I holler on my way back to her room. "I need a ride over my momma's house."

"Damn, nigga. You just gone hit-n-run like that?"

I laugh at her silliness. "Ain't nothin' like that sexy, but today I got a lot to do," I lied. Truth be told, I ain't tryna be stayin' up over her house like this.

"Aiight, nigga. Let me put on my clothes and I got you. Then I'm comin' back and getting some rest," Beautiful said through her yawn.

As tired as I am, I know me and I ain't kmbout to go to sleep now. It's Saturday and I'm so glad to be out. I ain't trippin'. I got some new-new on the first day out and I feel good.

Chapter Twelve

God forgive me for not acting like I know I should be. Forgive me for behaving ungodly and unwise. I know I said I wasn't gone do drugs when I got out. I have been cussing a lot and actin' out of my character to the fullest. I have no excuse, therefore, God please shower your mercy and grace upon me. In Jesus' name I pray...

God knows I don't wanna go back down the same route but honestly, it's very hard and I see this once again. It's not like I be on some jail talk or jailhouse religion but it's so easy to get swooped up off your feet in this wicked world that we livin' in nowadays.

I'm feelin' guilty for commitin' adultery and how I did my wife Nelle. Yeah, I know she has been doin' me wrong too, but I can't look at her. I gotta look at me cause I have to answer to God alone. I knew once I got out all this stuff was gone really hit me hard and the real test would begin. One thing I do know is this: *No test, no testimony.* I am more than a conqueror in Jesus' name; therefore, although I fall I will stand back upon my feet. I refuse to give up, saying that I know it's easier said than done.

Chapter Thirteen

"Charles, Nelle on the phone for you," Momma screamed from her bedroom.

"Okay! I got it," I said. "Hello!"

"Yo' kids wanna come over there with you today."

"Alright, bet. Tell 'em they can come and spend the night with me and go to church tomorrow with us."

"I'll tell 'em. They done ran back in they rooms, playin' with they toys."

"Nelle, I'm sorry for trippin' out on you last night at the club."

"Yeah whatever. Don't be sorry. Shoot, you always sayin' *sorry*."

"Well, I am because I don't like to lose my temper. You should be glad that I'm sayin' sorry cause as my wife you shouldn't be havin' Niggas all over you. And I done heard about you and Quan, too.

"Nigga, ain't nobody messin' wit him," Nelle interrupted. "You gone piss me off wit' that shit. Ain't nobody got time for arguing. You gone get me frustrated."

"Well, what's new Nelle? If it ain't true, why is you trippin' and gettin' mad. Whichever way, just do you and Ima do me, woman, cause you ain't no wife, you a trife."

"I ain't no trife, nigga."

"Well, I can't tell. Anyway, I will be over here at my momma's so when you ready to bring the kids, just slide though here. I'm about to get dressed cause I'm fresh out the shower." *Click,* I hang up.

"Ima young hustler, I know the ins and the outs, the in-betweens aren't what it seems, it's more like ghetto dreams, plots and schemes, fakers wanna be on ya team, fakers wanna be on ya team," I rap out aloud a song off of Ruff Lyfe mix tape, *No Features,* which never did get to drop in 2012 because I had got locked up.

I've been writing all types of music and believe I can make it in the rap game. I don't know all the business aspects, but I do know I got just as much talent as any of these other rappers. Not tryna toot my own horn, but these Muskogee Cats who got CDs out are alright, but they ain't fuckin' wit' me. I'm bout to come up in this rap game this time, fa' sho. I sat around on lockup for three years and put a plan together and you better believe I'ma execute.

I said I was gone go back to gospel music cause that's where I started off at. I was around eleven or twelve years old then and that was around about the time Lil' Bow Wow had first come out. When I got to be about fourteen and started runnin' wit' a different crew, then I started other music. My crew end up coppin' the name Red Mafia, because everytime you seen us we were bloody red. We were the bike clique, as well, cause we rode around town robbin' people on bikes.

Not saying that as a good thing, but looking back on how stupid we actually were, I can thank God for His mercy and His grace. I'm sittin' here lookin' at Channel 6 news and two men just got killed when they ran into Ryan's Convenience Store off of 21ˢᵗ Street and HWY 69 in Tulsa.

That's just one incident, but there are so many others just like that. I ain't with robberies no more. I'm very sorrowful to everyone I've ever robbed, as well. If I could turn back the hands of time then I would.

I've done so much wrong that now I want to do what's right because the fact remains that I don't want to continue the vicious cycle I've been living in. Besides, I learned early that the game ain't nothin' bkut a shame.

Honk...Honk...

I get up off the couch to look at the window and there is Nelle's red Maxima. I open the door and go out to the car so I can get my kids.

"Hey kiddos, give Daddy a hug. I love y'all."

"We love you too."

"Go in the house and go get out this cold. Do y'all got y'all clothes for church in the backpack?"

"Yeah, we do," they both speak as they run into the house.

I get in on the passenger side of Nelle's car. "Nelle, you somethin' else, you know that?"

"Whatever," Nelle says while playin' with her ear with her right hand.

"Girl, what is you doin' out the house with those little ass shorts on and tank top?" My dick at attention now.

"I ain't goin' nowhere. I been at home chillin' so it don't matter.

"Well, it don't matter to me right now," I say as I grab a handful of her fat pussy and hold it and look at her in the eyes while she's lookin' in mine as well, but with a cocked face.

I squeeze her pussy.

"Don't be squeezin' my pussy, nigga. That shit hurts!" Nelle said.

"Well, don't be givin' up my pussy like you've been doin'. You my wife, so don't you think that that hurts me?"

"I *ain't* been givin' up no pussy, for one, and for two, can't nobody hurt you."

"Nelle, only if you knew the full extent of how badly I was hurt and broken-hearted then you'd really realize. No disrespect, Nelle." I squeeze her pussy once again. "Keep yo' damn legs closed unless you openin' em up for me. I bet you got dick'd down by some nigga last night."

"Nigga please. I left the club early and went home and went to sleep."

"That's a good one Nelle, but anyways, I'm 'bout to get back in the house."

"Alright, well you can come over to the house and chill with me whenever you want to."

"Yeah, I'm cool right now, though, 'cause you ain't actin' right and have to prove yo' self to me. I tried to work our marriage out but you kept playin' games. Now I'm out, you tryna make it work. Well then, show me by word and deed, not just lip service."

I open up the car door, get out and close it shut as Nelle smashes off, burnin' rubber up the road. I shake my head in disgust. This girl still ain't changed.

I've never caught my wife cheating, but I've noticed things that make it seem like she is. When she left me for that last man I didn't even know until we got into it about her going out to the club all the time, then divorce came up and I told her to get it. She told me to get it 'cause it's cheaper in prison. I told her the only way I will get one is if you've been cheatin' on me and sexual immorality is in the picture.

Well, I have she said.

Damn, this the first I done heard of this. How many times have you done this?

Twice, she lied through her teeth.

Well, who is it?

You don't know em and you didn't tell me for two years so I'll tell you when I want to.

I snap out of it and head into the house cause just the thought of how she dogged me out in prison gets to me.

"Charles? Charliah? What y'all doin'?" I say as I enter the house and shut the door behind me.

"We in here wit' Big Momma."

"Well, don't be keepin' her up in there."

"I'm up. I'm just layin' here," Momma says.

It's 2:00 PM now and I need to find somethin' to do with the kids today. I ain't got no more money cause I spent the $73 that I had on my card when I discharged. I don't want to sell drugs but I don't want to be broke either. I can't even buy my kids nothin' to eat right now and I am not gone be busted up. I know this music is gone jump off but I need some money right now. And whichever way I gotta get it, I will get it or at least that's how I feel now. I'm not talkin' bout jackin' nobody though, but sellin' somethin' is in my mind big time.

Monday, I'm gone try to get a job somewhere so I pray all will go well and I believe it will. If not, I hate to say it but I'm gone holla at 2 Sweet. I been knowin' 2 Sweet for a while. 2 Sweet is well known and respected as a hustler in Muskogee and if he messes with you, he messes with you.

He is tall, about 6' 3" tall, thirty-six years old, dark-skinned, and muscular shape like a football player. Matter of fact, he played for Oklahoma State University and was about to be drafted by the New York Giants until he injured his tendons in his right leg and was out for about six months. While he was hurt and couldn't play ball was when he started hustling.

When I met him, I was about twenty years old and on the run up in Tulsa off of Rockford Street, living with my cousin John Lowe. John smoked big crack and his house was a dope spot and real talk, 2 Sweet had the game sowed up.

"Have y'all already ate?" I ask my kids.

"Yeah, earlier we ate some rice, biscuits, and bacon that momma made us but we hungry again."

"It's some leftover chicken-n-dumplins in the icebox from last night if y'all want some," Big Momma said to her grandkids.

"Yeah! Yeah! Yeah! We want some chicken in dumplins, Big Momma."

"Alright, I will make y'all some and y'all can eat it."

"Okay," I exclaimed.

Momma kept the house very clean and she's always been like that. She is just like her momma, my grandma, when it comes to cleaning.

I grab the pot of dumplins out the icebox and place it on the counter then reach up above in the cabinet and grab three bowls.

"Momma, you hungry too?"

"Yeah, make me a bowl, too," she said.

"Okay, I will."

I grab one more bowl out of the cabinet. I grab four spoons out of the dishrack. I fill up the bowls with dumplins and put two bowls in the microwave at a time at one and a half minutes each.

"Food is ready, y'all come to the table," I say. The kids run in the kitchen from out of Big Momma's room. "Say y'all prayers, first."

"We will," they say.

My kids are one year apart and they love each other so much that they love to be around each other. Better yet they don't like being away from one another because just like all siblings their age they love to argue and boss each other around.

"Here yo' food Momma."

"Thank you."

"You're welcome."

"You know I got you and will do whatever for you."

"What you watchin' in here?"

"Some Tyler Perry play with Madea in it."

"Oh, well let me know if you need me. I will be in the kitchen eatin' with the kids." I say my grace.

Lookin' at my kids eat, I'm inspired to not go back to jail. I love these kids so much and they are very respectful. For some reason, when I was younger I thought that I couldn't have kids, but apparently I was wrong and glad I was cause I thank God for my seeds.

"Have y'all been doin' okay lately and bein' good?" Both of them nod their heads *Yes* while continuing to knock off the bowl of dumplins. "Those must be good the way y'all eatin' em so quick."

"Uh hun," my daughter says.

"I want some more," Charles says.

"Alright. Let me get it for you. Do you want some more, Charliah?"

She shakes her head *No*.

I warm up another bowl of dumplins for my son and give it to him then continue smashin' my bowl.

"I'm sorry I ain't been in yo' life like I should Charles and Charliah and I want y'all to know that Daddy is here for y'all and I love y'all always. No matter what. So don't let nobody tell y'all different."

"Daddy, we want you to stay with us," Charliah says.

"Charliah, it's not that I don't want to, but truthfully, me and y'all's momma are not on good terms right now. Y'all remember momma use to bring y'all to see me in prison all the time and then she stopped and I didn't see y'all no more until I got out. Well, she left me for that man and didn't want me no more since she had him. Her and I have tried to work it out but we have not been able to see eye to eye since then. I love y'all's momma and I always will, though."

"Well, Daddy, have you been prayin'?" Charliah asks.

"I have, but not like I should be."

"Well, I pray for, Momma, my brother, Big Momma, Papa, and Nanna all the time and I know God hears my prayers."

"He sure does, baby girl."

"If y'all are through eating, then y'all can go in there with Big Momma or in the front room to watch TV. I will bring y'all a Juicy Juice in there as soon as I put these bowls up."

"Okay," they say and head back into the room with Big Momma.

Chapter Fourteen

Charliah is somethin' else. I know my kids want their mom and dad to be together, but its some thangs kids just don't understand. My son Charles does not usually talk much on subjects like that even though I'm sure he feels the same. After a while, when I would call to talk to him, he would not even want to talk to me so I figured that he was mad at me. But then again, I guess that's how the boys are sometimes. Charliah always wanted to talk to me and usually repeated things to me that her momma said which was how I knew their momma was filling their heads up with bologna. I didn't even talk to Nelle much cause she jumped ship cold on me. Instead of talking to me on the phone, she put the kids on the phone immediately. She treated me like trash but my kids don't even know the full extent of this.

"No weapon formed against me shall prosper," I say out loud before I go into the room with the kids and my Momma.

"I'm about to call Brother Franck right quick."

"He don't know you out, either," Momma said.

"Nope. I ain't even called 'em yet."

"Well, you need to cause you know he gone be happy to hear from you."

Brother Franck I met in the county jail in 2012 and we have continued to keep in touch. He is from Africa—Ivory Coast—and someway he ended up getting married to a woman in Muskogee named Angela and Angela got him thrown in jail in cahoots with Angela's mom for a misdemeanor—Assault and Battery. Angela got rid of all his belongings, computers, clothes, valuable information—including his passport. Therefore, if he would have bonded out, then he would have had a hold to be deported. He ended up beating the case in the end. We were celly's for about three months and I believe that it was a God thing for us to be celly's because I've learned a lot from him. Since I've been gone he kept in touch with me and encouraged me to continue to push. He is a minister now and goes by the name Prophet Joseph-Israel. He lives in Germantown, Maryland and told me that if I wanted a new start that I could go up there with him.

I dial his number and he picks up the phone on the second try.

"Hello!"

"Brother Franck," I say.

He laughs. "Brother, brother. How do you do?"

"I'm doin' good. What about you?"

"Yes. I am busy," he says.

"Yeah, well I got outta prison yesterday."

"Awww, I'm so *happy* for you, brother. God is good. I will have to check my schedule so that I can come visit you."

"That will be good," I say. "Because, like I was tellin' you when we were locked up, I'm scared to go back to the old me. God knows that I truly do not want to."

"All will work out. His grace is sufficient for you. He will finish the good work that He started in you. Continue to push. Push. Push. I encourage you to not give up one bit.

He begins praying for me.

"I love you, brother, and I am here for you. I did not forget what I told you, either. I will do a whole album for you. But like I say, continue to push."

"I will Brother Franck and I love you too. Matter fact, after I get a few things together here I still want to move down to Maryland. In about a week or two I'm moving with my brother J3 in Tulsa so that I can get away from this Muskogee environment."

"Okay, good," Brother Franck says. "What about your wife and kids?"

"I don't know about me and my wife cause thangs ain't goin' well with us, but I still ask God's will be done. It's hard on me though. My kids are doing well. They are over here with me right now at my Momma's house."

"Well, tell them all I said *Hi* and I send my love."

"I will and I'm gone be keepin' in touch with you as you already knowin'."

"Yes, for sure. I love you Brother Ruffin and take care."

"I love you, too. And take care as well," I said then pressed end on my Momma's cell phone that I was using.

It is about to be 8 PM now. I actually want some weed again. The urge had come back again on me.

I call Monkey.

"What up? You ain't got no more bomb?"

"I got one blunt, rolled up, that I was bout to smoke," she said.

"Well, slide through and bring some drank, too, cause family tryna get his head right."

"Alright, bet. Give me about twenty minutes."

"Bet."

"I'm bored, Momma."

"Come watch one of these movies with me and *ya kids* and chill," she said.

"I am tired of chillin', Momma. I'm tryna do somethin'. I prolly will go with Monkey for a lil' bit when she come through here in a minute."

"You *supposed to* be sittin' here watchin' yo' *kids*."

"I know Momma, but I won't be gone a long time."

"Alright, I hope not."

"I won't."

I went with Monkey over her house and she braided my hair while we blew back and drank a couple Lost Lakes. She ran the scoop down to me about all that's been goin' on in the streets and how dirty that my wife has been doin' me while I was gone. A lot of stuff that I did not know but I figured was happenin' anyway.

She told me how the streets have changed so much that you can't trust nobody. Nowdays, in this game, you can't find 'em real. You gotta watch ya' own peeps 'cause they mind ain't steel. I couldn't help but think of an old song that I had written which hit the spot.

"Yo' wife been out here goin' live Ruff Dawg and I don't wanna be puttin' it out there like that but she grimy. She been going to the barbershop late nights boppin' on them niggas for bars and liquor. She done turned into a hoe. I'm only saying this because you deserve to know, FAM. I got my shortcomings, I know and I've done lots of things too but Ruff, my nigga, I'm really tryna change. It's like I been lost out here in these streets without you. You a real Nigga and I love you. You not just my first cousin, but my homie, my true friend," Monkey iterated.

"It's vice-versa," I say as I sit and ponder on what she just told to me. I shake it off and puff on another hit of this Purp then pass it to Monkey. I know she be on some bullshit sometimes so I gotta read through the bullshit.

All gone be aiight. No doubt. I'm determined to succeed and I refuse, *I refuse*, to let anything or anybody hold me back. Real talk. Looking back on my life, I've fell down many many times, but also I've gotten back up every time because God has been right here with me. I know He has a purpose for me despite all of this mess I continue to go through.

Chapter Fifteen

It's Sunday morning and we are getting ready for church at Cumming's Cole C.M.E. Church in Taft, Oklahoma where my sister Sandra Givens is the pastor. Her and her husband of twenty years, Dr. Reverend Fedro Givens, raised me, my brother, and older sisters since prolly round 1993. Rev. Fedro Givens passed away last year while I was in the penitentiary and it was very hard on me and the family. It was a complete shock. I had a panic attack that was so bad that I did not know what was going on. I actually thought that I had went crazy. Like someone who had hit some PCP and never came back is how I felt. The first panic/anxiety attack was so bad I thought I was about to die. I had to talk to the psych doctor but first I went to medical because I thought I was having a heart attack the way my heart was beating out my chest, it felt. I could not stop trembling and shaking. I was having cold sweats and all that. I was told by the psych doctor that I had what's called a somatic body experience and that's an experience I wish on no one. The panic attacks I had after that was scary but not like that first one.

I thank God for Fedro and Sandra who I did not call daddy and momma but that's exactly what they were to me and I'm thankful for them. No joke, they were quite strict on us growing up but I can see why now. I know I've got into a lot of trouble but if it wasn't for a praying family and a family who disciplined and lived by morals then I would have been worse off.

"Shake the shackles off my feet so I can dance. I just wanna praise ya. I just wanna praise ya," I sing along to Mary Mary playing in the other room where my Momma is at.

My kids are sittin' on the couch watchin' Scooby Doo. My Momma screams from the other room, "Charles! Y'all bout ready in there? It's 'bout time to go."

"Yeah, I'm ready Momma."

On our way to church I couldn't help but to think of all the times me and Nelle went to church as a family. I often wonder why I even waste my time thinkin' about her when she does not even care that she does me wrong. She the type who has sex with another and says I ain't did nothin'. Her conscience kills her all the time, but she lets pride get in the way and we all know what comes after pride—the fall.

"Come to me all who are laden with burden and I will give you rest. My yoke is easy and my burden is light. God loves you and cares about your every need. He said in His Word that He will supply all your needs according to His riches in glory. We as Christians have to believe the Word of God and apply it to each and every area of our life. For it is not just enough to believe in God because the demons believe and even tremble in his presence. Be not only hearers of the Word but doers of the Word."

I'm listening to my sister Rev. Sandra Givens and it's like every word that she is speaking is punching me in the chest. I know that God is speaking to me.

"The doors of the church are open. The altar is open for anyone who needs prayer, who has been convicted in Spirit, who wants to give your life to Jesus Christ, or if you just want to rededicate your life. Come, while the blood is running warm through your veins, for tomorrow is not promised."

Tears running down my face, I stand up and walk to the altar; spread my arms to the sky.

"I would like prayer," I say. "I been out of prison for two days and do not want to end up going back. I don't want to go back to my old ways, either. I've been heavily stressed going through ups and downs with my wife and feel that it's irreconcilable. I also know that God is the God of reconciliation and there is nothing impossible for Him. I honestly don't know what to do, pastor. But I do know I need help. I need guidance. I need strength."

"What is impossible with men is possible with God. Charles, God knows your heart; he knows your struggles and pain. He wants to heal you but you have to give it all to Him. Let go and let God. Let go and let God. I know it's hard but you have got to forgive so that you do not keep on letting unforgiveness and bitterness root up in you which only causes more problems. Anything God asks us to do He gives us strength to do it," Pastor Givens said as she began to pray for me.

After church, we all go out to eat at Golden Corral in Muskogee off of Shawnee. My Momma, my kids, my sisters, my brother and nephews and nieces. We had a good time together fellowshipping with one another and talkin' about the good ol' days of the memories we had together. Then we all split up and go our separate ways.

Me and my kids go back to my momma's house and watch *Big Momma's House*, the movie together. I've watched it plenty of times and so have my kids, but that's what they wanted to watch so I was cool with it.

The whole movie I was sittin' thinkin' 'bout what went on at church and that I do need to forgive my wife and put it all in God's hands. When we take the kids back home I'm gone holla at Nelle on some real stuff and let her know that I will make it work or at least that's what I tell myself. It's obvious that I love her black tail and want us to keep our covenant. We can make it passed the sexual immorality and disrespect, I convince myself.

"Charles and Charliah, are y'all ready to go home cause y'all got school tomorrow."

"Yeah, we ready."

"Okay, well get y'all stuff and put it all back in ya backpacks and I will let Big Momma know that we ready."

"Momma, will you take me to take them home?"

"Yeah, is y'all ready?"

"Yeah, we ready."

"Okay, let me use the restroom and here I come."

"The next time y'all come with me, Daddy should have some money so we can do more stuff, but I'm just now getting out so I don't have much. I enjoyed spending time with y'all though and I want y'all to know that no matter what, I will always love ya. Grab y'all bags and I will walk y'all in the house 'cause I need to talk to y'all momma anyways."

I ring the doorbell once…twice…three times.

"Here I come," I hear Nelle say. "Come on y'all. Come in," She says to the kids. I smell liquor on her breath and her speech is slurred so I know she is high off those pills. She's lookin' all nervous.

"What you lookin' all nervous for?" I say.

"Ain't nobody lookin' nervous."

"Yeah, whatever," I say as I start walking through her house.

"What is you doin' nigga?"

"I'm checkin' out cha house. I ain't walked around in it so I'm tryna check it out."

"Well, you don't needah go back there," she says.

I look in the first room on the right which I could tell was my son's room. The door next to it was shut so I opened it which I could tell was my daughter's room.

"Charles, you act like you lookin' for somethin'."

I don't say nothin', I just open the door on the left side and was hit with what smelled like badussy—booty, dick, and pussy.

"You been in here fuckin' ain't you," I said.

"Nawll, I ain't been doin' nothin'. Don't start that shit Charles. I ain't got time for it."

"Nelle, you always sayin' that same stupid ass shit, as if I'm some stupid ass nigga. Ya bed all messed up and ya prolly gotta nigga under the bed or hidin' in the closet *right now*. Matter of fact..." I start walkin' to the closet to check it as she jumps in front of me.

"Charles don't!"

"Move bitch," I say as I throw her on the bed.

I open the closet door. "Who the fuck is this nigga, bitch?"

"Uhm, uhm…" I grab her by the throat.

"Let me get up outta here," the nigga said who I didn't know.

"Yeah, get up outta here, 'cause this *my* wife that you fuckin' on. I should beat yo' ass but I know how playas rock. It's this bitch fault 'cause she still bein' triflin' like a hoe."

The nigga ran up out the house. He must have walked or somethin' cause it was not a car out there. The garage door was closed so I knew my wife's car was in there or at least I assumed.

"How stupid could you be, Nelle? You still on this bullshit but steady hollerin' you wanna make us work. From now on, miss me because I been done killed you and all these niggas you fuckin' with and be right back in prison while you fuckin' and suckin' on 'em again. Therefore, bitch, do *YOU* from now on. I came here to make up our relationship but now, *hell nawll!* I hate you, bitch," I say as I leave up out her room, seeing the kids watching.

"I'm sorry Charles and Charliah for reacting like that. I love y'all and will talk to y'all later," I say while giving them a hug. I smash out the house and get into my momma's car. The look on my face told it all.

"I saw that man comin' outta there. Who was that?"

"Some nigga she in there fuckin' and suckin on! Fuck her! Let's ride out, Momma!"

"Don't you get yo' self in no trouble foolin' wit' that girl, Charles. I'm tellin' ya. If that's what she wanna do then let her, but you ain't gotta be mean to her and cussin' her out."

"I'm tryin' not to momma but it's hard when you've been with someone so long and they continue with the bull."

Chapter Sixteen

I see right now that I gots ta get up and outta Muskogee, ASAP, before I get myself into some nonsense. Right now I feel so much hate in my heart. It is what it is though. Fuck all the bullshit. I learned from an old school potna before in jail, he said to me, "Ruff, if you continue to lower your standards, you soon have no standards." Thinkin' on that is some real shit and I'ma stick to my guns and keeps it pushin'.

It's Monday mornin' so I got dressed to impress to look for a job. I put on a pair of these khaki Dickies pants, this white short-sleeved polo button up collar shirt, and these all-white Nike Air Max shoes on my feet. I went to Action Temps, Express Personnel, and Command Staffing to put in applications. I went to a few restaurants including McDonald's, Sonic Drive-in, and Burger King, but to no avail. I was told the usual line that they like to give a person who has a felony record (and on top of that I got braids and look thuggish, at least that's what I'm sure they think), *we are not hiring at this time.*

I seen 2 Sweet at McDonalds off of 32nd Street while filling out an application and he gave me his number and told me to call. He said that he wanted to talk business wit' me. I really aint tryna get back into the game but like I've said time and time again, I don't like being broke.

I seen Jo-Jo and he told me that he got the rap game poppin'. He told me all I gotta do is get at him 'cause he is performing at clubs, throwin' concerts and really making it pop on the rap tip.

I got JoJo's info from him cause I had lost touch with him for a while. He had moved back to Omaha, Nebraska and I heard that he was getting in trouble down there so he came back to Muskogee. And me, well, I've been in and outta lockup as well since we caught that case with A-City. A-City got smoked in 2011 I heard. He kept on with the grimy stuff and it ended up costing him his life. A-City had actually wrote a statement back then on that case blaming it on me and JoJo—mainly me—because I was the youngest and he was facing a life sentence for habitual criminal. But you know how the game goes. You live by the gun, you die by the gun.

My sister, Meik Meik is taking me to get a cell phone at 5 PM when she gets off work so I will go to Boost Mobile to get one. In the meantime, I'm gone sit here at the house and write a rhyme while listening to some old instrumental beats that I been having before I went to prison.

I gotta do somethin', bein' broke I ain't wit' it,
I need it in a major way, Ruff, I gotta get it,
I'm goin' thru a lot but, no, I won't complain
Ima warrior, Ima solja, it's a must I maintain...

When I got my new cell phone I locked in the numbers that I had from peeps I was locked up with as well as my family and old acquaintances. I got on my Facebook page and looked at all the drama that was going on on there and also locked in with some of my peeps that I ain't heard from or seen in a while.

Man, what type of business could 2 Sweet have with me? I'm wonderin'. All I can think of is he must got a package for me. And even though I kept sayin' I whatn't tryna sell no drugs, man, I needa get on my feet, so fuck it. I dial 2 Sweet's number and he picks up on the second ring.

"Who the hell is this?" he speaks in a harsh barbarous voice.

One thing 'bout 2 Sweet is he does not like to answer numbers that are unfamiliar because of the snitchin' that has been goin' on rampant in the City of the Gee.

"It's ya boy, Ruff Dawg," I said. "What's good with you, homie?"

"Oh, my bad, homie. I didn't know this number so I whatn't even gone answer but I'm glad that I did."

"Well bro, lock me in cause this is my new number."

"Okay, bet. I got cha now, dawg. It's now after nine PM and I close down all traffic at this time so tomorrow at noon I want you to come by my house. I live on 16th Street between Court and Emporia in the two story house on the corner. Ain't no way that you can miss it. You will see my 2013 Benz on the dooky-dukes outside."

"Okay, bet homie! I will holler at you tomorrow then."

"It's on. Take it light, nephew," he said as he hung up the phone.

I call JoJo and let him know that I'm down with the rap game and I let em know that I have wrote lots of stuff while gone. I've written more than I've ever written before and I'm ready to make it pop. He told me that he has a studio in his house and that I'm welcome to come over anytime that I would like. I let him know that I'm down with it and within a couple days I would drop through over his house which is on 18th and Denison across from 18th and Denison Church.

I spark up this half blunt that I have from earlier while thinkin' bout all that's happened since I got out. Things are so much different this time cause I ain't been single in so long but I actually love it and feel extra free. I feel that there's no stoppin' me. I mean I ain't concerned wit' females like that anyway cause they come a dime a dozen. Ms. Beautiful is the only chick I done knocked off so far which was basically on a hum-bug but it is what it is. She did have some bomb pussy and head game though.

I see now I gots to get at these hoes somethin' crucial. These hoes love the Kid and I love that they lovin' me. I love how I get to have bitches on bitches on bitches. What I really love is now I'm single so I mingle.

Chapter Seventeen

Today's a new day and I'm tryna make somethin' pop. I'm ready to move up to Tulsa with J3. I'm gone give it another day or two then I'm gone. I look at the clock and its 11:30 so I go head and pat-n-turner to 16th Street so I can holla at 2 Sweet. My thoughts racing about what it is he could have for me. Whatever it is, I'm gone appreciate it, that's fa' sho, 'cause this walkin' round and catchin' rides from people ain't my style. If I'm tryna ride out, I'm tryna ride out. Most definitely not be waitin' 'round.

As I approach 16th Street I see the Benz that 2 Sweet was talking about on the phone. It's very clean, exactly like he said. All black with the tinted windows, exactly like I like it.

Outside is a pretty blue pit bull that looks like it came from CAM kennels which is my brother J3's pit bull line. 2 Sweet came outside on the porch to greet me and told me to come on in.

"I was sittin' waitin' on you," 2 Sweet said. "You should have called and I would have come to pick you up instead of you walkin'."

"I didn't mind, man. I'm use to walkin'," I said. Sittin' in his front room I could tell that 2 Sweet was doing big thangs. He had a 75 inch flat screen TV on the wall with surround sound speakers all around the room. A black leather couch with a matchin' love seat in which his girl was sittin' on lookin' fine than a mug like she was right out of Victoria's Secret magazine. She had red lingerie on that seemed to be screamin' my name. I know she could tell I was checkin' her out but she acted like she was fully dressed which told me that she was used to it. She was Hawaiian and Puerto Rican with long hair exactly like I like my women to have.

2 Sweet went into a different room and come back with a brown paper bag and tossed it to me.

"What's this?" I said while lookin' inside.

"It's you, my nigga. I just wanna look out for you to help you get on yo' feet since you just now getting out. That's two ounces of ice and two ounces of powder. Five racks so that you can have some bread in yo' pocket. I don't want nothin' in return so don't trip. I know you might not want to get involved in this and if you don't then no pressure. You can keep that paper and give me back the drugs, but if you want, then do you bro."

Yeah, I really whatn't tryin' to sell nothin' and said, "I whatn't but I needa get it 'cause I need it in a major way right now." I gave him dap. "Good lookin', homie. On the real."

"It ain't nothin' Ruff. You know I fuck with you the long way."

"Most definitely."

"I got some blueberry weed if you smoke."

"Hell yeah," I said. "Twist up."

"Aiight, bet. I already got one ready to blow but I will give you a half just on the strength. I'll be right back." He left, then came back in the room smokin' on the blunt and threw me the bag of weed. "The streets ain't the same, homie. The game ain't nothin' but a shame. Therefore you gotta keep ya eyes open, bro."

"Fa' sho," I say, hittin' the blueberry weed which tasted delicous.

For I know the game is a shame but I know I gotta do somethin' to get me and my kids up outta this struggle, therefore I'm neck deep in it now. *I'm 'bout to make somethin' pop,* I tell myself in my hustler motivation attitude.

Me and 2 Sweet sat and chop it up for at least an hour before he took me back to my Momma's house. I felt so good because of the quantity of product I had that's all mine that I actually gained an ego immediately. At the same time I felt that I was just like all the other cats who be locked up talkin' 'bout what they ain't gone do when they get out but go right back to it, which makes it true that cats that be locked up mostly be spittin' jail talk.

The thing about it is, we don't always mean to not keep our word. We be really feeling that way at the time, but sometimes thangs don't always go as planned.

"Fuck it," I say. "It is what it is. I'm not 'bout to sit here and beat myself up. I'm gone get thangs to movin'."

I call J3 on the phone. "J3, what's good bro?"

"Chillin', bro! What's up, wit' it?"

"I'm still tryna come down that way and I holla'd at my potna 2 Sweet and he looked out on me on some stuff so I'm gone put you on too and we can get it poppin'. I got a lil' bread so I can gone buy a lil' whip to push around. I prolly be up there Thursday or Friday."

"Aiight," J3 says. "Just holla at me. It's on bro."

I really don't even know where to start with this work cause I been gone three years, but then again, I'm gone make somethin' happen cause I gotta get it. Let me call JoJo before I go to sleep.

"JoJo," I say as he picks up the phone on the 3rd ring.

"What up Ruff Dawg?"

"Sittin' here thinkin' bout the come-up. Like I said, I'm tryna get it in with you in the studio. If possible, I would like to get in there tomorrow."

"That's what up. Come through," JoJo said. "Matter fact, Saturday at nine PM I gotta perform live at Max's Garage and want you to be there with me and even come on stage wit' me as a feature."

"Okay. Bet, homie. You knowin' I'll be there. Tomorrow I'm gone come through and we can lay one down specifically for that night."

"It's on. Holla back."

"Yeap."

It's now time for me to call it a night. I been goin' at it all day. Tomorrow I gotta busy day. First thang, I needa locate a vehicle for about $1000-$1500 so I can get around more easily.

Chapter Eighteen

My dick rock hard as I open my eyes. For some reason I had a dream that I was fuckin' the shit out of Candy. She was goin' live like some shit you would see in a porno. I ain't tryna cut that bitch but I know I'm gone knock somethin' today, I tell myself as I hop out the bed and stretch.

Thank you God for another day.

I check my phone and have a couple missed calls and text messages. I can smell my Momma in there, cookin' breakfast. It smells like my favorite which is rice, bacon, and biscuits and of course a glass of milk.

Before I eat I take a gangsta while lookin' on my Facebook page on my phone. I then hop in the shower, brush my teeth and get dressed. I put on my all-black Echo suit. The Echo sweatpants and the hoody sweatshirt with an all-black t-shirt underneath. My shoes are all black Jordans. My hair is still fresh from when Monkey hooked me up and the beads are still dangling.

All of Monkey's lil' friends be tryna throw me the coochie but I don't always bite cause some of those hoes be easy and I don't like it when it's just too damn easy. But today, I ain't even trippin'. I'm gone knock somethin' off proper.

I know JoJo is prolly up so I'm gone go over there early this morning and we gone blow some of this blueberry and make a hit.

"Momma, will you please give me a ride to the store then over to JoJo's?"

"Okay," she says.

I grab some regular Swisher Sweets, two boxes, and a six-pack of Budweiser in bottles. To my surprise, JoJo was already in the lab when I got to his house.

"What's poppin' bro?" I said.

"Checkin' out these new beats and getting in the rhythm of thangs, dawg."

"Fa' sho. Well, twist up one of these blunts," I say.

"Awww, this beat go hard homie. Let's write something to this. I'm already thinkin' of somethin' hot. Check it."

Fire in the buildin', no drop and roll.
Sexy lil' mama shakin' ass on the pole.
She got me on bulge, she got me on swolle.
I'm doin' my best not to lose control...

"That's *straight* right there dawg and it's definitely somethin' for the club," JoJo says while splittin' the Swisher Sweet with his thumbnail.

"That's just somethin' quick. I don't know about that one exactly though, cause in a way I would like to do somethin' more cocky, like this old song I wrote called *Feelin' Myself*. It's simple. It goes:

I'm feelin' myself, I'm feelin' myself...
Feelin' gooood, feelin' gooood...
I'm feelin' myself, I'm feelin' myself...
Feelin' gooood, feelin' goooood....

"Okay, let's go wit' that one," JoJo says.

"Bet, homie. Just throw a verse on there and I already got two verses that I will rock to it."

"It's on," JoJo said, inhalin' the marijuana smoke from the blunt that he just lit.

"Here's a beer, bro," I said.

"Bet," JoJo responded through coughs.

"Pass that shit if you can't handle it," I joked wit' 'em. "I smoke on nothin' but the best, my nigga. You know me."

I pop the top on my second beer.

"This is some bomb, Ruff Dawg. Where you get this from?" JoJo says as he passes it to me.

"The homie 2 Sweet chunked me a half of this yesterday."

"Fa' sho, fa' sho. Let's get back to this music."

We bob our heads to the beat while drinkin' and smokin'.

"This is what I got," JoJo says.

> *Muskogee is the city, we reppin' fo' the town.*
> *In the 9-1-8, you know it goes down.*
> *You know we act a fool, you know we act a clown.*
> *Ain't no need ta ask, in the Gee it goes down.*

"Hell yeah, my nigga. I'm diggin' that. Matter fact, I got a verse that will go perfect for that song."

"Aiight. We gone do both those songs this weekend," JoJo said to me with a big smile on his face.

"JoJo, you know I'm 'bout to be movin' to Tulsa with J3 very shortly. I was gone go in the next couple days. Most likely I will just wait til' Sunday since Saturday we got to show up and show out at the Garage."

"Now that's what I'm talkin' 'bout," JoJo said, liftin' his beer bottle in the air as to a toast.

"Most def," I say, lifting my beer bottle in the air while nodding my head in agreement.

My phone rings. I check the caller ID. It's Monkey. "What up, Monkey?"

"Shit. Over here at the house chillin' wit' my homegirl, Mini. She the one I was tellin' you about that was goin' crazy over you when I showed her some pictures of you."

"Oh yeah! Well, if she lookin' good, I just might knock it off."

"She's pretty. You know I ain't gone be tellin' you nothin' bout no ugly female."

"You bet not," I said. Did you get some moe bars, yet?"

"Yeah, I got some."

"Well, I got some bomb so come over here to JoJo's and pick me up and I'ma chill with you and Mini for a while. Oh, and have you heard of anybody sellin' a car? I'm tryna buy one."

"Ima make a few calls and will let you know when I pick you up."

"Bet," I say as I hang up the phone.

JoJo steady bobbin' his head and writin' some lyrics before I interrupt him.

"JoJo, I'm waitin' on my cousin' Monkey to slide through and pick me up. Ima be ready for this weekend. Maybe Friday or Saturday we will rehearse all the way through the two songs if need but if not we will just rock it."

"Aww yeah, most def," JoJo says, still noddin' his head to the beat in concentration on what he was writing.

I've been over here at JoJo's for about three hours now and am ready to move around. Actually, I'm tryna be around some pussy. Mini or whatever her name is I'm ready to check herout. If she is alright, I just might put her down on my team. Not like us being together or nothin', but someone I can kick it with tough. I'm cool on a deep relationship status 'cause dealin' wit' Nelle was a lot and I ain't tryna be tied down. *I'm bachelor status and I'm proud of it*, I say to myself as I nod my head in agreement and lift up on my nuts. Besides, I'm tryna run through lots of these females that I turned down last time I was out tryna be Mr. Faithful. Fuck that faithful shit. It's my time to live life to the fullest without bein' tied down. Real talk.

"I'm diggin' that beat, homie. You make it?"

"Yeap, you knowin' I'm a beast when it comes to layin' these beats down, Ruff Dawg."

"Yeah, you always have gone hard at that and spittin' the lyrics."

JoJo actually went so hard when we were younger that I wanted to rap like he did. When it came to freestyling he could spit fire and I can honestly admit that the reason I got so good when I was young was because that's all he ever wanted to do was freestyle. I had got to be just as good as him or better at age seventeen or eighteen but after that I slowed down on freestyling and began to write more rhymes down than just freestyle them. Me and JoJo had put prolly three or four songs together, maybe more. The only thing about them was that the chorus was wrote and the verses were only freestyle.

But the songs still sounded alright.

"I just do what I can," JoJo said. "Besides that I get better by working with you and other great artists like you."

"Already," I said, lookin' out the window cause I heard a horn. Sure enough I see her black Chevy Caprice with the none-ya-business tint like I like my vehicles to have the windows mob'd out. "It was good to stop by and mess wit' you homie. I'ma be ready for this weekend. If you need me, just gimme a call."

"Okay, fa' sho," JoJo says as we dap each other up and I head out the door with my last beer in my hand.

I get in the backseat of the Chevy. "What's up, fam? Mini? Y'all doin' aiight?" I speak to them both, at the same time noddin' my head to them as both of them are lookin' at me. I close the door.

"Chillin', fam-bam. Just so glad that we can chill together like old times. I be needin' you out here wit' me," Monkey says as she takes off drivin', turnin' up the music just a notch or two.

Tunchi's back, Tunchi's back...
All these bitches yellin' that—
Tunchi's back, Tunchi's back,
Tunchi's back...

"Already, fam. I'm back for good this time. No doubt. I see this is ya friend Mini you were tellin' me about."

"Yeah, this homegirl and she a down ass bitch too, my nigga. Fa real."

"Is that right?"

Monkey didn't tell me that Mini was white, which doesn't matter but she could've told me cause I assumed she was black with the name Mini. Mini looks like a J-Lo or a Katy Perry mixture so I ain't trippin' instill. Mini is very sexy. She looks more like a college girl, not someone that would be hanging with my cousin Monkey, but hey, it is what it is.

I wonder if Mini gotta fatty in them jeans she got on. I can't see much while we riding in this car but when we get out I'ma be checkin' her out from head to toe 'cause I'm diggin' what I see so far. She got her long brown hair pulled back into a ponytail. I can tell that she's a lil' bashful, but that's all good. Ima fuck that shyness right up outta her. Yeap. Ima beat that pink-toe up. Ya heard me.

I laugh to myself 'cause I be thinkin' some crazy stuff but, hey, Mini is gone get da *business*.

Chapter Nineteen

Today we gone show out at Max's, me and JoJo. A lot's done happened over the last few days. I bought an all-white immaculate Cadillac DeVille sittin' on 22 inch rims, which got me feeling like David Banner. The windows are five percent tinted and two fifteen speakers got the trunk pounding. I'm proud of this car, on Momma's.

The work game I'm pushin' hard. I went ahead and utilized what 2 Sweet gave me so I got it poppin' like a mu'fucka, now. Mos def. *Look at me* is how a nigga feel, fo' real. To all the ones who showed me no love when I was gone, I'm showin' my ass for y'all. Y'all must've thought I'd be down forever, but never that. I'm back.

Oh, you prolly wonderin', ain't you? Well, yeah, I knocked ol' Mini off. Mini got a mad head game on her. She's a Go-Live'r. That's why I had to chop it up with her and have been since that day. She about money though, and she has been bringin' some cash in. If it don't make dollas, it don't make sense. I needa get paid and that's all that's on my mind.

Right now, I'm stackin' up. It's love out here in these streets, just like suppose to. But, hell naw'll I don't trust these niggas or these hoes 'cause I done learned my lesson too many times. But I am runnin' into some good people and opportunities and I'm gone execute on them because it's my time to ball.

The last couple days I been runnin' through the females, though. I ain't braggin' but I done prolly hit fifty different pieces of coochy. That's prolly not a lot to most but bein' that so much time I been off the streets due to lockup I done missed out a whole lot. Then again, not really cause ol' Nelle was my boo and I really wanted us to pop but she chose up and it wasn't wit' me, but wit' the next man, so...

One monkey don't stop no show. What I do, I go harder and continue pushin' and I push because of people like her who gave up on me. For all the naysayers in this world period, I'm goin' harder than ever.

I'm blowin' back all day like I was before I got locked up. Ain't many people smokin' on Reggie. It's a lot of loud around. Best believe that's exactly what this is, right now. This that purp. The real purp. Not that bull people be callin' purp. It tastes good and it don't take a lot and you be good than a mug.

I holla'd at my P.O. yesterday and let him know that I'm gone be movin' wit' bro so I got dat locked in right there. I hooked J3 up wit' a quarter ounce of what I got so he could do his thang. Besides, wit' bro it's all good cause it's all in the family.

It feels so good to be free from those prison walls cause that stuff was literally for the birds. In truth, not even for the birds, because even they deserve to be free. Now, freely, I can move around, get on my cell phone wit' out sneakin' round, and I feel good. I feel like the song says; *Feelin' like a million bucks...*

I ain't even been out seven days yet but I been kickin' it. I done hooked up wit' a lotta homeboys and homegirls that I didn't talk to when I was gone. I know the outta sight—outta mind thang, but as a grown man—or better yet, mature adult—you realize that life goes on. You don't trip just cause people didn't write you or put money on your books or visit you or any of that. You just realize that it is what it is.

Now I'm back in circulation. It's definitely what it is.

I ain't trippin' on nothin' petty. I'm just tryna have a good time and take care of business like never before. I believe that I'm wiser than I've ever been, speakin' mentality wise. I know that this life is real and in life there are twists and turns. Sometimes we get hit with things that we never saw coming and sometimes it's repetitive that we go through the same thangs.

We live and we learn is how I look at it so I'm just tryna improve. I know that I'm sellin these drugs, but it's not anything permanent. It's just temporary until I get my paper right and start this business of selling clothes, shoes, merchandise, etc. I continue to follow my dreams so to speak because I believe that if a person has realistic goals, then they can be reached. A person also has to first believe in themself, and I definitely believe in myself.

I believe in God and all that and I stand on his word. When I say stand on it, I mean if it says it in the Word, to me its Gold. You can't knock me off my rocker tryna convince me it's false.

To some, they can understand where I'm comin' from and some can't. I am not meaning to sound hypocritical, I'm just sayin' straight up that there are some things that I know I should *not* be doing, but at this moment, I'm smashin' the gas.

I been choppin' it up wit' my fam, Poopie, lately and I sat him down with a lil' work 'cause he is about his money. I love family, big time. Lil' relative looked out for me plenty times while I was locked up, too. I definitely appreciated it too, cause when a brotha is gone due to lockup, he is usually forgotten.

I've been scopin' out the scene down here in Muskogee and it's changed a lot. A lot of new faces in the town. The youngstas out here wild'n out, but the OGs just sittin' back. Instill, they are gangstas so you knowin' they will still get ill. A lot of the young bucks think us G's don't still go hard, that we done went soft, but we just got wise, that's it. We will still tear some shit up.

It seems that people are tired of doin' time so they are keepin' they noses clean and I don't blame 'em. The MPD is still thick than a muthafucka down here in this small town. I know ain't no way I'm tryna fall victim to they human warehouse system. Not no more, anyways.

Chapter Twenty

♫ ♪ ♫ ♪
♫ ♪ ♫ ♪

The ladies in here thick and they pussy poppin'
Like the switches on the chevy, they are tail droppin'
Vibe along to the beat, yeah body rockin'
Nonstoppin', I can't help myself from watchin'...

♫ ♪ ♫ ♪
♫ ♪ ♫ ♪

I done slid up in this club and it's packed already. From the sexy ladies to the fellas, it's deep in here. It was hard to find a parking spot outside as well. *It's gone be easy to get off this product I got tonight*, I say to myself as I scope out the scenery.

Disco lighting, bobbin' heads, beer bottles, liquor cups in hands. Everybody dressed to impress and from the looks of it, everybody is just tryna have a good time. As I approach the VIP section I see JoJo who is smoking on a blunt and noddin' his head. I feel like all eyes are on me in here even though I know it's prolly not. I feel like Tupac when he was sayin' some shit like that.

There's plenty of my niggas in here. C-4, Lil' Rick, Notch, A.P., Shot G, Spook, Lil' Dawg, Marlo Mike, Trillville, Sid Kid, Geezy, L.B., C-Nutz, Twin. That's just to name a few of my niggas who up in here.

"What's good, JoJo?"

"What up, Ruff Dawg? You ready to show out in this muthafucka?"

"You betta believe it dawg."

"Show up, show out, show up, show out," JoJo says passin' me the blunt. I take a few hits and pass it back. I swallow the rest of the Grey Goose I got in my cup.

"Get ready, get ready! For our feature presentation tonight we have JoJo and Yung Ruff, two local rappers representin' right here from the City of the Gee. Give it up fo' em as they drop some flavor in ya ear."

The crowd is goin' wild and I'm feelin' my adrenaline rushin'. "Let's do this, dawg," I say to JoJo as I grab the mic off the stage.

"Check one...Check two... What up wit' it tonight? Hope er'body enjoyin' themselves and havin' a good time cause that's what it's 'bout. Now I'm gone have ta tell y'all to turn up wit' me. One love."

The beat drops.
>*Slurr'd speech, bloody eyes, lookin' like they asleep,*
>*Poppin' bars, blowin' blunts, nothin' but that sticky skunk,*
>*Hennessey got me drownin', I be lost in the lake,*
>*I don't know how much more of this I can take...*

I'm high, I'm drunk, I don't even give a fuck,
I'm rowdy, I'm bowdy, chunkin' middle fingers up,
Whoever don't like it, feelin' froggy? then jump!
I got my dawgs wit' me, no leashes, no chains.

I love the reaction of the crowd. It's all love in here and they are feelin' this song, too. A simple hook, but catchy.

I'm feelin' myself, I'm feelin' myself,
Feelin' goooood... feelin' goooood...
I'm feelin' myself, I'm feelin' myself,
Feelin' goooood... feelin' goooood...

It always feels good when you got the whole crowd rappin' your song wit' you. It makes you feel unstoppable. This is only the first song. The one I put down, but we gone do JoJo's as well.

I ain't wit' the slippin', mega grip monkey bars,
Facin' the moon while lookin' up to the stars,
Airplane high, won't let you take me below it,
Flute in the room, I guarantee I won't blow it.

Needle and thread, a miracle I start sewin'

> *Reapin a harvest while outside it is snowin'*
> *It's dark in the room, no lamp on, I'm still glowin'*
> *Walkin' around like it ain't nothin', ass showin.*

> *Blowin' grass all day, like I'm a human lawn mower*
> *New chick couldn't blow, my old chick had to show her*
> *Just wanna be down. Don't even care if she score*
> *At first at the front, she want me at the backdoor*

> *I'm feelin' myself and I ain't talkin' 'bout lotion.*
> *Bringin' me down, you might as well keep hopin'*
> *Keep on coastin', ya vague plan won't work*
> *Ima fighter, I fight until I get put in the dirt...*

As much love as it is in here, its equal hate in here as well. I feel the tension risin' from these hatin' ass niggas whose female keep on gawkin' and eyeballin' me and my dawg JoJo while we up here puttin' it down. Therefore, I sense the duel and if one of these bitch ass niggas try me tonight they gone get it.

This bitch Nelle in the crowd all bar'd out and stumblin', hollerin' *that's my husband, that's my husband!* That bitch needa stop that shit ASAP cause she ain't mine, she's a rat and I hate to be like this but fuck it. She disrespected me too much while I was down so fuck her and she still on that trifelin' shit. Like the sayin' goes, "I can do bad all by my damn self."

She can stay on those niggas she been on who wasn't doin' nothin' but usin' her dumb ass and breakin' her. She was so blinded by the drugs and dick that they were puttin' on her that she can't have my dick no more. I honestly wish the bitch wasn't my kids' mother.

Yeah, as you see, I get pissed off even seein' the bitch, that's why I gotta get to Tulsa to get away from her.

"Muskogee, Oklahoma in the buildin'. Muskogee Roughers, STAND UP. We representin' to the fullest. It's ya boy, Yung Ruff, wit' my Dawg JoJo and we came to give y'all a good show because it's all about y'all."

"Fa' sho, fa' sho. Y'all heard it right," JoJo said. "And that's the reason we dedicate this final song to y'all. 9-1-8 in the buildin'," he says as he lifts his fist up in the air.

Muskogee is the city, we reppin' fo' the town.
In the 9-1-8, you know it goes down.
You know we act a fool, you know we act a clown,
Ain't no need to ask, IN THE GEE, it goes down!

Of course it goes down, round afta round
Four pound packin', I ain't wit' the actin'
Eyes stay open, 'cause these niggas stay scopin'
Tryna come up, on a easy ass lick.

And I ain't goin' for it, I press fast forward
Headed toward the prize, and it ain't no surprise
In the Gee it's all gas, you a get GAS'd up,
Get blasted up and put in a casket.

Yeah, this song a lil' harsh, but it's reality
Yeah, them heads are bobbin', hands wavin' in the air
In Muskogee, Oklahoma we just do not care
And we ain't the type of gangstas who be blastin' in the air...

I got a potna name Smudgy Blacc from O Killa City who I was locked up with two different times. That nigga goes gorilla on the rap tip, but he's more into the gangsta rap and he would always say to me, "Ruff, be aggressive on the mic everytime," and that's exactly what Ima do everytime is be aggressive. At the same time, he told me to make sure I enjoy myself and have fun with it.

Fuck these hatin' ass niggas in Muskogee besides all these bitch ass niggas do is give me fuel and motivation to make it and I will. I will make it out this no good game, believe me.

"Good performance," JoJo said.

"Same to you homie. We did our thang tonight. I felt the love at the same time felt the hate from these niggas in here."

"I did too," JoJo said as he shakes his head and bites his bottom lip while crackin' his knuckles. "Fuck these niggas, homie. They ain't talkin' 'bout shit," he continues. "Let's roll up and grab a drink."

"Okay bet," I said, givin' JoJo some dap as we head back to the VIP.

"That sounded real good," 2 Sweet said, cheesin', showin off his all-gold grill with diamonds blingin' in each one.

"Appreciate that homie. I didn't even know you were gone be here."

"What! Homie, you shoulda knew I was gone be here, besides everyone has been talkin' bout this and I had to support you, bro. I'm here for you to the fullest. How you been doin', Yung Ruff?"

"I've been doin' good. Steady pushin' and tryna enjoy myself to the fullest as much as possible. You know, tomorrow I'm gone be movin' to the Thug Town wit' my bro, but mos def I will be back and forth."

"Well, homie, keep in touch wit' me and know its real wit' me," 2 Sweet said as we shake each other's right hand and lean in to hug on another with the left arm.

"One love," I say.

"One love," 2 Sweet repeats.

As I enter back into the VIP section, I feel a lil' uneasy, like somethin' just ain't right. I don't know exactly why I'm feelin' this way, but my senses are right eight times outta ten. I mean, nothin' looks out of the ordinary, but instill…

The music is mellow in here as the DJ got Dream *Rockin' That Shit* playin'. The dance floor is packed as the ladies and niggas alike ran to the floor when it first came on. It's some fine ass women in this bitch tonight too, I must admit. I must admit that I'm feelin' good too, especially after that performance that we just did.

Fuck you nigga, you ain't talkin' 'bout shit! You mad 'cause yo' hoe want me. That ain't my fault. You need a be checkin' her 'cause she the one choosin' and in violation of you, not me, playboy, so get it right...

"What up! What up!" I say, snappin out of the daydream to JoJo passin' the blunt to me. "My bad homie. I was in a daze fo' a second."

"Yeah, I can tell," JoJo said. "Say dawg, do you see them two cats over there by the bar?"

"Yeah, what about em?"

"Well, those niggas keep lookin' over this way and whisperin' to each other as if they on some sneaky ass shit. And I don't trust these niggas. They look too suspicious."

"Do you wanna push up on em, dawg?" I say.

"Hell naw'll," JoJo snaps. "That ain't the way we do shit now days, dawg. We bosses and we play shit a whole different way."

"I know, but we can't let them niggas get up on no bull while we ain't lookin'. Therefore, we both gotta keep our good eyes on 'em."

Passin' the blunt back, I stand up, stretch, and take a big gulp of the vodka that JoJo had got fo' me and head to the restroom. "I gotta piss homeboy. You cool 'til I come back?"

"Handle yo' business, homie. I'm Gucci, believe me, dawg."

"Hey, baby!" Nelle says to me as I pass by her. I ignore the bitch and keep pushin' to the restroom. *Fuck all that baby shit*, I tell myself. I ain't got time for it.

I push the restroom door open, thinkin' to myself, *what type of bullshit this drunk-ass woman on? 'Cause I ain't got time fo' her tonight.* I piss; wash my hands and head back out the door.

"I know you heard me, Charles!" Nelle says.

"I ain't heard you say nothin', Nelle. What's up?"

"I just wanna talk to you and see what's up. I enjoyed you up there."

"Appreciated, Nelle, but me and you ain't got nothin' to talk about like that. I love you and always will, but besides that, we ain't got nothin' in common no more. I mean our kids, but that's it. By the way, you needa get yo'self together cause you—don't take this as bein' rude to you or being disrespectful—but Nelle, you are the laughing stock of the town. You steady lookin' fo' love, pleasure and comfort like that's all there is in life and it's more to it than that. I hope the best for you Nelle, and I'll holla back."

"So you ain't gone hug me or gimme a kiss? Nothin'? It's like that?"

"It's just the way you made it when you forgot about me in lockup and told everybody that you wasn't wit' me. You bein' my wife you was pose to ride fo' me and you didn't. It is what it is, though, so... I'm out, Nelle."

"But...I...I..."

"Bitches ain't shit," I say out loud as I smash off from Nelle.

What the fuck is goin' on? Is that JoJo? Hell yeah that's JoJo ova there. I run over to VIP. "What the fuck is this, dawg? Do we have a problem, homeboys?"

"Yeah *we* gotta problem and it ain't got shit to do wit' *you* unless you wanna make it somethin' to do wit' you," one of the two dudes said with a mug on his face and liftin' up his shirt showin' a gun.

"This my nigga and its whatever. Why you gotta show a pistol, like you gone do somethin' wit' it?"

"I will nigga," the same dude said, steppin' into my arm's reach.

"Chill out, Loco," the tall dark dude with platts in his head said grabbin his homie back.

"Fuck you, nigga. You ain't talkin' bout shit. You'se all bark, NO BITE."

"We'll see about that! We'll see about that, bitch ass nigga!" Loco said, backin' up into the crowd with his homeboy who had him by the arm.

"You okay, dawg?" I say to JoJo.

"Yeah, I'm cool, dawg. I guess these niggas is trippin' bout some bitch that I fucked two weeks ago that apparently was Loco's baby mama. I didn't even know it though and don't even know Loco or the other nigga or even know how they know me besides Daydrionna must've told her nigga. But whichever way, these bitch ass niggas is in violation how they pushed up on me and especially Loco for showing that gun."

"Oh yeah! They gone get it!"

Apparently this was the niggas who were muggin' earlier. I'm listenin' to JoJo while I'm thinkin' to myself how I could've got shot or anything just for helpin' out my homeboy, which always seems to happen wit' me. A crowd has drawn around now, bein' nosy, tryna see what's goin' on. I'm feelin' a bit antsy now and ready to get up outta here and do somethin' different. I've never been the crowd type who likes to draw attention to myself even though I have been the type who has been known around town and in the streets.

"Fuck it," I say. "Don't trip, JoJo. We gone take care of these mark ass niggas. But right now, let's finish this night off wit' a bang."

Chapter Twenty-One

Heading out the door of Max's, I run into Candy who is lookin' sexy as ever. I mean, she is lookin' ten times better than usual and she's already a dime. I know she is a rat, but man, this rat got me wanting to gun her down. Nevermind all those nasty dick ass Summit niggas who done been up in her.

"Hey, how you doin' Charles?" she said in a nonchalant type of way.

"Hey Candy," I responded, lookin at her fat ass which immediately gives me a boner.

She watches my eyes as they go from her eyes to up and down her body. Her curvaceous hips screaming out my name from underneath the light blue jean skirt she is wearin'. A yellow pair of Jimmy Choo pumps she sports on her feet are splashy, along with the yellow V-neck t-shirt to match that reads *Meow* across her breast in big black bold letters. As much as I want to get up under her skirt, I keep it pushin'.

Outside in the parking lot there is lots of people standing round drinkin', smokin', choppin' it up and doin' what we know it to be called as parkin' lot pimpin'. Head nods and peace signs I receive as I head to my Cadillac. I get in and start to thinkin', Man, *here I am at this club and already got beef with these cats over my homeboy. I ain't tryna be back locked up—but fuck it. It is what it is.*

Its fun livin' this life, but then again, I know it's not something that I should keep doing. This night got me really thinkin' 'bout sayin' forget all the drama and hype.

I have not been reading my Word like I was for at least the last six months of my incarceration. I had backed up from the cussing and drugs but now it's like all that stuff is threw out the window. I feel as if I'm full fledge back in the game. Okay, at least knee deep, though, not neck deep or I wouldn't even be thinkin' like I'm thinkin' right now.

I start my vehicle then push back to the house to get some sleep.

Chapter Twenty-Two

Today I'm makin' my move outta this town, I say to myself with a big smile on my face. I'm excited about going to the Thug Town but then again, I don't know many people that way, which is actually good so I'm ready. Besides, I gotta few potnas from there, already. Plus the ones I've been locked up with, so it's gone be cool.

It's this one female I use to talk to when I was sixteen at Rader named Lil' Bitt. Lil' Bitt was chocolate skinned, long hair, with a fat booty and big titties that matched her five foot four frame perfectly. She would push up on me tough and I would turn her down again and again until one day I said *forget it*. Not that she was not a sexy fly chick, but the games those broads played at that facility I was not trying to be a part of. Besides, the women were very few there—at the most, fifteen—and it was two hundred plus men, so you do the math. Those chicks had like ten niggas chasin' 'em down and fallin' in love and all that weirdo stuff that I was not tryna fall victim for.

I had a potna name DeMario Clayborne who was in love wit' this girl named Gina Kelsey and, boy oh boy, that nigga would go *bonkers* over her! Crying in his feelings, feeling some type of way, fo' real.

Anyways, Lil' Bitt is a hustlin' ass chick and I know I could prolly hook up wit' her down there and get somethin' crackin'. Then again, times change so ain't no tellin' what type of shit she on.

B-Moore is makin' some moves with those white people down there in the Thug. I'm definitely gone fuck with him.

Poopie, Monkey, and Mini, I'm gone keep in the game in the Gee as long as they keep up the stroke. I won't have to worry about Poopie, but Monkey and Mini I will. Now, I *do* trust Monkey, cause she my fam, but she likes to get messed up too much and that right there is a sign of weakness. I mean if you too drunk to function and too bar'd out to remember, then you could easily become a victim.

I got all my stuff boxed up and ready to go, so I will head out after church in Taft, today. My brother will be there too, so I will follow him back.

My mind is racin' and I ain't even got out of bed this mornin'.

If it don't make dollas, I'm Gucci on that,

I'm Gucci on that, I'm Gucci on that.

If it ain't about real shit, I'm Gucci on that,

I'm Gucci on that, I'm Gucci on that...

The ringer goes off on the phone and I look to see that it's Monkey. "What could she want this early?" I say out loud then press Talk.

"What's good, FAM?" I speak.

"Chillin'. Was wantin' to know if you heard what happened last night outside of Max's about 2:30 in the mornin'."

"What happened?"

"JoJo got shot two times in the chest and once in the leg by some cat they say name is Loco. Jojo is in critical condition and was life-flighted to Tulsa. Loco is on the run, the police lookin' for him. They say his real name is Perry James from Louisiana. He been down here in the Gee for the last two or three years though," Monkey said.

"Okay! Well, whatn't nobody else involved in the shootin'? Cause me and JoJo got into it with that nigga Loco and some other cat that he had with 'em last night about one or one-thirty, then after that I rode out cause I wasn't feelin' it."

"Naw'll, I think it was only him from what everybody says, but the word is that his homie he was with was Tommy Shaw and he whatn't tryna have no problems. He was really tryna keep Loco outta trouble, but Loco don't listen to nobody. He's messed up in the head, fo' real."

"Yeah, well if they don't get Loco befo' I get to him, then this is gone be a closed case cause Ima knock that nigga off for this one. That bitch ass nigga raised up his shirt, flashin' that pistol at me last night too."

"Ruff, I know you heated, but you gotta stay out the way. You just got out and I don't wanna see you gone again from out here wit' me. I need you out here FAM, like a muthafucka, cause you keeps me level. I be lost without you. I told you."

"Yeah, I know Monkey, but fuck all that bullshit. Well, Ima get dressed and go from there. Hit me up if you hear somethin' new."

"Love you."

"Love you too. I'm out."

That's crazy how that happened right after I left. I felt somethin' whatn't right. I should've told JoJo to get up outta there when I left, then maybe this would have never happened. JoJo wouldn't have been slippin' like that, I know. Especially knowing that we just had got into a confrontation with them cats so it has to be more to the story. I hope ain't nobody had him set up, then again, it could have been that the nigga Loco was waitin' in masquerade.

I can picture that snake ass nigga in his vehicle with some binoculars, lookin' at the entrance door of the club, waitin' anxiously but patiently until he seen JoJo comin' up outta there. The last thing on JoJo's mind was some shit like that, I know, unless he would've been prepared.

The nigga Loco was already dressed in all black in the club. He had on an all-black hoody with black Dickie's pants and a pair of all-black Reebok Classic shoes. I could see how furiated he was in the club and knew that he had murder on his mind when he lifted up his shirt showin' off what he was packin'. At the same time, I didn't think that nigga was really gone be doin' some shit like this.

Them bitches get so many niggas fucked off by either getting 'em locked up or the niggas doin' somethin' stupid to get locked up behind the bitch, or somethin' along those lines. Look at what this nigga did over his lil' female just because she gave another nigga some pussy. Niggas gotta be smarter to stop trippin' with the nigga when it's the bitch who is bein' faulty, not the nigga. I mean, unless it was ya homeboy or family. Then that's *different*. But instill, the bitch should have mo' decency and respect for you and herself to not scoop that low.

Bitch, you ain't gotta call my phone. Matter fact, all you hoes can leave me uh-lone!

"Hello!" I say as I answer the phone.

"What's good, Ruff Dawg? This C-Nutz. Everybody was sayin' you and JoJo got shot last night at the club. I didn't know what was up."

"Naw'll, it whatn't me, homie. But I did just receive a call from my fam, Monkey, sayin' that JoJo got shot three times by a nigga name Loco that we had a lil' run in wit' last night, but I ended up bonin' out early."

"Have you heard how JoJo doin'?'

"From what I hear, it ain't lookin' too good. He's in critical condition and was life-flighted to Tulsa."

"Oh. Well, I wanted to call and check on you, dawg. If you need me, then holla at me."

"It's on, homie. Holla back," I say as I press End.

I go hop in the shower and once again my thoughts begin racing. Now folk got my name in they mouth, big time. Word on the streets is always somethin' else cause Muskogee talk so damn much and over 80% of the time they don't even know the facts.

I hear my phone ringin' but until I get out this shower, I ain't concerned.

All I can keep picturing is Loco shootin' my homeboy as he was not expecting it. Two bullets in his chest and one in his leg. I wonder where this coward ass nigga Loco is right now. He knows the police are on the hunt for him so I know he is hidin' out but, boy oh boy, I want this nigga Loco dead, not locked up. I usually don't even think like this but fo' my dawg JoJo, I'm wantin' this nigga Loco to pay.

I get out the shower, put on my Ralph Lauren Polo pants that are black with gray stitches. My black and brown Polo boots I put on and a black Polo collar t-shirt that my sister Meik Meik had bought for me. She bought it the same day she bought me this Apple touchscreen iPhone 6 cell phone that I got.

"Hello!" I say.

"What's good wit' it, FAM? It's Poopie. I know you been hearin' what's been poppin' in these streets."

"Yeah, I heard," I said. "It's messed up too, but that's how the streets is."

"I know, Ruff. You know they had yo' name mixed in all of it too."

"Yeah, I heard all that bull homie, but really it had nothin' to do wit' me. I was just in the club and seen two cats pushin' up on my nigga JoJo and whatn't gone let him get jumped. A lil' bit after that, I smashed out."

"Well FAM, I wanted to let you know I got this change for you and I'm ready to re-up."

"Okay. Bet that. I will slide through." I hang up the phone.

I got bout an hour befo' church starts so Ima slide out and make a few moves right quick. First thang first, I head to my car and put my boxes in the trunk that concealed my clothes, shoes, hats, CDs, pictures, all my lyrics, and of course my laptop with my recording material.

"Did you get all ya stuff packed, Charles?" my Momma asked in a helpful, but depressed type of way.

"Yes, Momma, I did. You know, I really want to stay here with you but it's gone be best for me to go up there wit' J3 so that I can stay away from this Muskogee nonsense."

"Yeah, I just want you to be careful, Charles. You know I worry bout you."

"I know, Momma, but I'm gone be okay."

"Are you gone be at church today," she asked.

"Yes, Ima be there, Momma, so I will see you there. I'm 'bout to make a few moves."

"Okay."

Smokin' on Purple ease my mind,

This that shit that we get high to...

(yeah)

Murder, murder, murder, gotta keep your nine...

Boosie came through on the speakers as I started the 'Lac. I dial Monkey's number. "Monkey, I'm on my way through," and she said *Aiight*.

As I arrive over Monkey's, I notice a few extra cars over there. I'm not too much of a people person and ain't tryna be bothered this mornin' with all this stuff on my mind. I ain't trippin', though, cause I mess with people at the same time, just prefer not to right now.

"What's goin down, Ruff Dawg?" Matt P said, comin' out the door to greet me.

"What's happenin' FAM? It's been a long time since I seen you. How you been doin'?"

"I'm good. In Texas, makin' this money and stayin' out the way. I only come to Muskogee on occasion. I heard you were out and I'm glad I get to see you," he said as we both give each other hugs.

We head in the house which I see Monkey sittin' on the couch with her two kids. Beasta is sittin' on the opposite couch with his wife.

"What's up wit' it, FAM," I say, lookin at everybody so that they know I'm addressing them all.

"We just sittin' here chillin'."

"That's what up. Well I ain't got long then I'm headed to church then to the Thug Town wit' J3, but right now I'm tryna roll this L up if y'all don't mind."

"Hell yeah," Monkey said. "Twist that shit up. Oh, and I got that bread for you that Mini dropped off to me. And I got mine too and we ready to get on again, FAM.

The customers is lovin' that shit and it's been sellin' like hot cakes."

"Alright, just gimme the money and maybe later on or tomorrow I will put y'all back in the game. I need you to hit Poopie up fo' me, too, and tell him I'm ova here if he wants to slide over and drop that paper on me."

"Okay, I got ya, fam."

"What's been happenin' Beasta?"

"I been workin' and keepin' my ass outta these white folks way. I ain't been havin' time to do nothin' else because I get it in so much at work."

"I'm glad to hear that FAM, 'cause we ain't tryna be locked up no more. Ya feel me?"

Beasta is doin' real good. He don't drank no liquor no more. He use to love that Wild Irish Rose wine. As cheap as it is, that stuff use to keep that red ass nigga on one. He was definitely a bald head nutt. He stands about my same height, around 5' 6" tall and is literally red-lookin'.

I love family. Him and Monkey are brother and sister so they both my first cousins and I'm close to both of them. They got an older brother name Rico who I love, but we ain't as close. He is a preacher and a business man. He getting gwap through cutting grass, he got a Subway, and he be messin' wit' that cattle. He got so much goin' on that he is straight, but boy! — He what they call *TIGHT*! I mean *tiiiiiiiigghtt*!

Matt P is my guy. I call him FAM, but we ain't blood FAM. We grew up together when I was younger though. Matt P was a pretty boy back when we were in school. He kept the waves 360 bangin' with the tapor fade and thin side burns. I remember when we first met in 2nd

grade. We were both going to Irving Elementary on the eastside. We both loved track and were two of the fastest at the school and that's how we came to be cool wit' each other. We were about the same speed. Sometimes I would beat him and other times he would beat me but it was all love. Also, it was this girl name Amber Falcon who was top notch then, and it was his lil' girlfriend. Well, everyone wanted to get at this girl and she ended up breakin' it off with him for me. That had Matt P real salty, but still he didn't trip like that.

I can still picture him when he came up to me after class and said, *Man Charles, she broke up wit' me. She said she messin' wit' you now. Is that right?*

It is but it ain't like that, Matt.

I ain't trippin', whichever way, Charles. I hope y'all the best. I ain't no hater, besides, it's hundred's of females at this school.

It's kinda funny thinkin' bout that but hey, that was back in the day.

"People outside," Monkey said.

"Dang, he here quick, ain't he?" I said. "Here, fire this L up," I said, tossin' it to Monkey. "Have you heard anythang else bout JoJo?"

"Naw'll. Not yet, but everybody say he might not live."

"Damn. I'm gone have to visit 'em when I get to Tulsa, if possible."

"Naw'll, they said only immediate family 'cause it's been people already trying."

"Oh."

"What's up, everybody?" Poopie said as he came in the door, clean from head to toe in his colors, blue and orange. He had on a pair of six inch Timberland boots with a blue pair of Levi's 501s with a Denver Broncos football jersey on.

I puff on the L as I stand up and show love to my FAM, Poopie.

"You tryna touch this my nig?" I say.

"Yeah, let me touch it bro, befo' I skirt out. I got my baby mama in the car. I was just stoppin' by to drop you this bread. I'm gone be ready to re-up whenever you ready or back in pocket, so holla at me." He reaches in his pocket and hands me $4,000. "Who's this on?" He says, passin' the blunt to Monkey who had her hand out lettin' him know its back on her.

"Ima get back wit' all y'all," Poopie said as he heads out the door, and back into his car.

Lookin' at the G-shock watch on my wrist, its 10:45 so I'm bout to skirt out myself so I can get to church. "Let me hit that L one mo' time, and then you can get it," I say. "I gotta go ahead and get to church."

Passin' the blunt back to Monkey, I give her a hug and tell her I love her.

"I love you, Matt P. I love you, Beasta. Fam, y'all get at me sometimes."

Chapter Twenty-Three

As I enter into the parking lot of Cummings Cole C.M.E. Church, I hear the music playin'. It sounds good. I can tell its Uncle Tony cause he got that distinctive voice.

Let the Church say, AAAAA MEN!

Let the Church say, AAAAA MEN!

I realize that if I don't stay involved with church or stay in tune wit' Christ then I will be slidin' farther and farther away from the change that I desire. I know gangbangin' ain't for me, but I'm still considered one. I mean I still wear the colors and prolly always will. I stopped smokin' weed but now I'm full fledge back on it. I've been cussing like a mug, lately and back livin' a worldly life.

When I come back into the presence of God I can't help but feel remorse for my behavior. Now I'm back out here on these streets and I sometimes feel that I did all the soul-searchin' in vain. I can say that I have grown though. When my wife left me it made me truly reevaluate the lifestyle I was livin' which I knew I shouldn't have been livin' in the first place but it opened my eyes to crunch time. I knew I had to make a change cause I was tired of walkin' with cement in my shoes.

Wherever there is opportunity, there is opposition. I received opposition from many of people, but I know I have to live my life and accept the consequences that go along with my choices. I know that things will get better or at least that's what I tell myself. I do know that anytime we give up somethin' that is dear to us or that we are attached to then we go through a period of suffering. Therefore, I come to realize that some suffering is good. Now the suffering is not always pleasant, but it is necessary for growth.

The church house is packed today, which is a beautiful thing because on the average prolly only twenty people be at church a week, but today it's prolly a guestimation of fifty.

I sit in the third pew from the front of the church, next to my Aunt Connie who is rockin' side to side and clappin' her hands—all off beat.

I bow my head to pray. *God, I thank You for Your love and Your mercy that You show to me. Forgive me for backslidin' and fallin' off track since I done got out. I need You bigger than ever cause I cannot stay focused without You. I feel that I cannot change, but I also know that feelings are not facts. On top of that, God, You are with me and with You I can do all things. This game ain't nothin' but a shame, God, and I know it, but I have to admit that somethin' in me is still hooked on this life. I shouldn't be, so God, I give You me so that You will change me completely and make me whole. Thanks for my family and friends, God. Keep JoJo in Your arms, Father God, as he is in critical condition in the hospital right now. In the name of Jesus, I pray. Also, keep me in Your Arms, Father. In Jesus' name, Amen.*

I can feel the presence of God in here. It's love in here and I feel it like I haven't felt in a long long time. Prolly since I was around eleven or twelve. Ya see, I grew up in church since at least age six, therefore, now at age twenty-seven, it's still the same. I always lean on God and I know He is real. If it wasn't for Him I believe I would've been dead or been done had a life sentence.

I remember days and nights where I was itchin' for a body. I remember when I got hooked on cocaine. I was puttin' it up my nose on a daily basis. Around the age of twenty I started doing Primo's and soon after that I was smokin' on the pipe. I went from sellin' it to doin' it wit' the clientele.

I remember one time in particular that I went to sell some crack to a dude I had been dealin' with named Carl. Carl was around forty somethin' and I knew him because he called his self an OG Blood and me bein' a younger homie from the set, we linked in. One day he called me for a 40 so I took him some over to his house. I ended up smokin' some out of his pipe wit' 'em and sold him somethin' fat for $40. It was greed made him want the prolly eight-ball that I had left and he pulled a gun on me and said give it all to me befo' I blast you. I looked him in the eyes at the same time lookin' at the barrel of the gun that he had pointed at me. I said, "Are you serious, homie?" He repeated again, "Give it to me, before I blast you." I threw the dope at his feet and left up out of the house, thinkin' how close I was to getting killed over some dope. I wanted to say *Hell, Naw'll*, but my life meant more to me than that dope.

I had at least a six month run on smoking the Primo's strong before I had gotten locked up. Getting locked up was a blessin' in disguise, because I was on the verge of killin' myself in that lifestyle. Of course I wanted to stop but I was addicted to that stuff and if I would not have gotten locked up I would've been still goin' hard prolly, or more than likely. We all have struggles, but to put them out in public view takes courage.

I have to be honest that all the jail time and prison time that I've done has saved me. It was God savin' me because I know He has a plan for me. Even now with me playin' the hot, cold, up, and down route that I have been caught up in since I can remember. The last lockup that I did I grew more in Christ than ever before and I thank God for that. I know that He will finish the good work that He started in me cause He is the author and finisher of my faith.

"Praise the Lord, oh my soul. His praises shall continually be from my mouth. His Word moves me, soothes me, and behooves me. I love the Lord with all my heart, mind, body, and soul. For God is good, God is greeeeaaatt!" the preacher, Rev. Sandra Givens says as she stands at the pulpit. Her long black hair has blonde streaks and is pressed down, hangin' past her shoulders. She is wearing an all-white women's suit Jacket and a skirt that matches along with a pair of white high heels.

"If God be for us, who can be against us, church? Time is short and God is coming back soon, lookin' for a church without spot or wrinkle. I don't know about you but I wanna be ready and I do believe you are ready or that you wanna be ready, unless most of you wouldn't be here in the house of the Lord. I say *most* cause you know some folk just come to church to show off. Some come to impress someone else, rather it be Momma, Daddy, girlfriend, or boyfriend. Whoever! We as a whole have got to get it together. Encourage one another. Pray for one another instead of hurting, condemning and critisizin' one another."

"It's a lot goin' on in this world! From shootings to killings! Burglaries to robbings! Kidnappings to rapes! Drug addictions! Homosexuality! Et cetera! Et cetera! You fill in the blanks but you know what yo' vice is and what it is that gets you or at least you need to know so that you can be on guard against it. Everybody has different weaknesses in this world and I said all that to say…"

"We are overcomers in the name of Jesus Christ because He overcame the world and we are coheirs with Him. We are overcomers by the blood of the Lamb and the word of our testimony. Therefore, we have the same power within us that He had and He said that *we* would do greater things than He did. Resist the devil and he will flee. Folk now days don't resist. When you resist, you feel some tension, strain, and if ya not careful, then yo' mind will tell you to stop resisting because yo' body and mind is uncomfortable. But sometimes we need to be uncomfortable for a while cause, as you see in certain circumstances, it's good and beneficial for yo' growth."

"In closing, if you ain't got no struggle or conflict that your dealing with yo'self, then maybe you needa pick a fight with yo'self. Find out what it is that you got goin' on that is keepin' you stagnant."

Listening to the preacher as she preaches puts me in a mind frame of change. I know that I could put this rap down fo' the gospel and touch lives because the streets is definitely needin' a Gospel Avenue to bring thugs, gangstas, criminals, prostitutes, drug addicts, and sinners into repentance. Someone that knows their struggle, their pain, and been-there-done-that so that they will feel connected through the music and at the same time, come to know Jesus Christ as their savior.

I've always been a visionary and I can see it happenin'. I can also see some other visions in my head. Some legal and some not so legal or should I say, some Godly and some not so Godly. I'm just sayin', cause I'm human and I'm gone make mistakes. Nobody's perfect. Ain't that what people say when they caught up in somethin' they know they ain't got no business doin' but to justify it they got an excuse that involves, *God know we gone sin.*

Sad to say, but its truth that that's how I feel now. Not all the way, but if not careful it could go from minimum to full blast in no time therefore it's a must that I get the Word in me.

I can't help but think what's goin' on with JoJo. He's been my Day-One so long that I don't wanna lose him. Church is about to let out so as soon as it do I'm gone call Monkey to see if she has heard anything. It's hard to concentrate with all that's on my mind but that's a part of the process in life so I'm just takin' it in and not getting ahead of myself.

I talk to a few people, mostly family, after church is over. I hop in my Lac, thinkin' heavy. *What is it gone take for a nigga like me to change?* I mean like really, *really* change, cause it seems I won't ever just do it. I know right from wrong. I know about God, but none of this stuff seems to keep me on the straight and narrow.

Chapter Twenty-Four

I check my phone and I see several missed calls and a few text messages.

- He didn't make it- the first text message said that I read. I had to take a deep breath hearing that. Ridin' in my 'Lac, I fire up the L that I rolled before leaving Church. I'm followin' J3 to his crib so I can put all my stuff up and start from there.

I grab my CD case and grab Plies and listen to *One Day*.

Wish I could bring my nigga back for one day,

And take him by the daycare to see his son play,

And go to show him how his baby momma done went stray,

And how them fuck niggas who claiming they love you done walked away…

. Tears I shed fo' my dawg and hate that this happened but one thing fa' sho is JoJo will always be in my heart. I remember when we first met in 9th grade. I was fourteen years old. JoJo been my dawg *tight* since day one and truly is my Day-One nigga. We done had good times together and bad times. We done even fell out for a while but we made up and stayed down with each other.

"This some bullshit," I say out loud as I throw six quarters into the change catcher at the highway tollgate. I hate this shit is happenin' like this but one thang I ain't gone do is allow grief to kill me. I have learned over the years that it's a time fo' everything. I learned that grieving is good but too much and it can destroy you. I learned this when my brother-in-law Fedro passed away. I guess you never know how close you are to someone until they die and that's fo' real. I knew I was close to him but not so damn close to have a panic attack and I know I ain't tryna have another one and be stressin' over somethin' I can't change. One thing I will do is get up on my shit to the fullest, fo' my boy JoJo, Fedro, and all the ones that I've lost.

Ima make this rap thang *boom* and get this money by *all means necessary…*

Chapter Twenty-Five

Six months later...

Since I hooked up with J Serious it's been goin' down on the rap tip. I got a double mix tape that drops in January and it's gone be hot, cause I'm hot in this game, right now. 2 Sweet dropped me off a key of cocaine and I ain't looked back since, which has been four and a half months ago—give or take.

Me and bro J3 is goin' hard together and I'm lovin' it. We got twin Mercedes Benz and when we pull up we shittin' on 'em like geese do and you know they got some green stank bombs.

I ran back into T in Tulsa and put him on. We bumped back into each other at the grand opening of the strip club that me and J3 own called Skinz. I wasn't tryna get him involved with this movement knowin' he had just gotten out recently, but he said he was tryna get it so I had to put my dawg down. T had gotten a lot more buff from when I was in the penn with 'em. I was glad to see my dawg, too.

"I thought you was out preachin' or somethin', Ruff Dawg,' T said.

"I prolly should be," I told 'em, "but right when I got out, I couldn't get a job and needed to do something to get the paper. My potna put me on and I just kept on pushin'. I'm preachin' that a nigga in for a rude awakening tryna stop my shine." We laughed together.

T gave me his number that night and we stayed locked in like when we was in together.

Skinz is gone be a successful venture I'm knowin' cause we got the finest ladies in there, music, drinks, live performances, and all. The name Skinz let you know that it goes down at this place.

I've been out round bout a year and I am blessed, seriously. Money is not a hassle for me like it used to be. I use to be ready to kill for money, now it's a whole different ballgame 'cause I'm runnin' through paper.

I bought this house in Tulsa in the same neighborhood my brother lives in off of 41st and Garnett. The perfect dream home for me cause it's my first house I've ever owned. It has three bedrooms and 2 baths, a double car garage, and fenced in gate. My kids love it and I got both of them spoiled and it feels good for me to be bein' a Daddy for once.

Being a dad is a great joy to me and everyday I'm learning more and more how to be a good dad. I get the kids on the weekends and when they are not in school. I want to get 'em permanent but their mom isn't goin' for it. I hate that things are like this, but the chips have fell were they have fallen and I'm just playing my position.

We have a court date soon on legalizing this divorce and makin' it final. Truth be told, I'm ready cause it's been a long two years goin' on this breakup. Lookin' from the inside out, I see that I'm now livin' life and now that I'm living life, there are obstacles and challenges that I have to face. I have to man up.

It's harder on me mentally than ever before but at the same time it's copacetic. I'm enjoyin' everyday life although it's so much that has changed in the last five years that it still gets to me.

Financially, I'm strapped up, though. I bought my mom a 2016 Lincoln which is all-black, 4-door, and has some 22" rims on it which are factory rims, but they are clean. You should've seen her face when I pulled outside her house in it. Walked right up to her as she sat on the porch swing gettin' a breeze with her drank in her cup, relaxing.

"How you like that car, Momma?"

"It's nice."

"Well, it's yours, Momma," I said, handing her the keys as she jumped to her feet immediately and gave me a big hug and a big kiss, then she ran screamin' out loud *Thank you, God! Thank you, God!* I was just glad I was in a position to buy her a new car.

Those times like that, I'm proud to be part of. To be able to bring joy into someone's life that I love is an amazing achievement. To see them smilin'.

I was able to give my sister Nicole $10,000 dollars to help with the four kids that she got and I told her *don't worry 'bout givin' it back, that's what family is for.* I know she needed it so it was no problem and me I'm all about family first. I believe that families need to get together more and discuss real life issues more with one another. I want the whole family or team to be makin' it and if we keep our heads put together we can all thrive to the top.

It's still some things I don't understand in life, but I guess that's part of life. I've always been the type to think. It's not a day that goes by that I'm not thinkin' *Why this? Why that? How come?* Like that. *What did that mean? It's gotta be somethin'*...

I rationalize to myself that I will slow down on this hustle but right now I'm getting it in from three or four different ways. I ain't been to church in the last six months, though I do pray to God.

I just been livin' a Dough Boy life; Rap Star life. If it ain't right to live like this, then I needs help tremendously, because—no lie—I love this shit. From where I come from, it's like I'm in Paradise er'day.

No joke.

Chapter Twenty-Six

It's just another day in my life of makin' money.

I got to be at the video shoot at 4 PM and I'm ready. I've got my apparel picked out, already. My hair is braided up and I got my beads danglin' just like I like it.

"It's gotta be the prime of my life," I say, opening up the refrigerator and grabbin' the last *Lost Lake* outta there.

I need to re-up on these dranks. I started drinkin' *Lost Lake* beer in 2011 when I was out the last time and it's stuck on me. I like that it only takes bout 2 or 3 and you good and buzzed. I have to admit though I drink them back to back and be pissing all day.

I spark up the half-blunt in the ashtray from last night, kick my feet up on the table, and relax on this leather couch listening to *Block Nigga,* the song for the video shoot.

> *I'ma Block Nigga, keep me a glock, nigga.*
>
> *Hustler gotta keep me a gwap, nigga.*
>
> *It's in my veins, block life 'til I drop nigga.*
>
> *Born in the 80s, I was raised as a Block Nigga.*

I'm just picturin' the scene and I know it's gone be jumpin' fo' real. This is like the third video shoot I done did and it's always a blast. I done created a buzz so big that it's nothin' but love. My hands are busy makin' it happen and I thank God for it all. I know this would not be possible without him.

I remember watchin' all the rappers, singers and actors on TV like *Yeah, I'm tryna do that* but I didn't know where to start. Now I see that there is a way to get there even if you live in Oklahoma where it seems hardly anybody ever makes it out. I know I'ma make it big though, because I feel it inside of me like I've never felt before in my twenty-eight years of living.

I feel unstoppable right now.

I am actually the business man that I use to only dream about. I didn't know how it would happen back then. Now it's here and I see it takes hard work at whatever you're doing and you definitely gotta have drive. You have to push yo'self because no one else will push you like you will push you.

How I feel right now is like Miley Cyrus. It's always gonna be another mountain. I'm always gonna wanna make it move. I can almost see it. The dreams I'm dreaming. I'm just enjoying the climb. Yung Ruff is steady puttin' the pieces to the puzzle together in this life, but I'm steady learning, so it's a process. As I continue with the process, the progress can't help but start to show beneficially.

I done came a long way but I know I still have far to go…

I thank God I am not where I use to be, though.

Chapter Twenty-Seven

LIGHTS...CAMERA...ACTION!!!

It's deep on the set. I mean it's lots of people here for the shoot. Everybody is dressed to impress.

We have about two or three different scenes in this shoot. We are here in Muskogee shootin' this video on 18th Street between Emporia and Denison which is just the first location. We right outside my sister's house which is right here on the block.

"Alright! Alright! It's time," the camera man Johnny says, who is one of the two video editors that we have on our team. Johnny is in his early forties and has been involved in this industry for the last twenty-four years; since high school. Johnny is short, slender and bald-headed and stays clean-shaved. This lil' Mexican means business all the way to the max.

I head into my sister's house which is where the video will begin. I will start here putting my money and gun on my waist. Headin' outside to the block where my homeboys are already posted up, waitin' on me.

I greet each one of 'em by handshakes daps, and hugs while we standin' on the block rappin' *Block Nigga*. Its women walkin' by—hood rats—lookin' and blowin' kisses at us. Niggas drivin' by muggin' out the windows of they cars, hatin' and shit. The police are ridin' by slow lookin' at us peeping what the fuck we got going on.

Everything is already planned out for each shoot and my crew has all of it mapped out and that's what they get paid for. To make the scene come to a movie view and keep it interesting and fun to watch.

I love the fact that the title of the song goes with the scene so well. I appreciate all the love and support because without my support team none of this would be possible.

The next shoot we will go to the Mall where I'm gone literally buy some new gear and pop tags. The fact is that I'ma Block Nigga, but I'm also a hustler and stayin' fly is mando.

During breaks we all smoke blunts and do some drinking. I'm not doing much drinking though because I have to be able to deliver. Besides, I already drunk a few *Lost Lake* earlier so I'ma lil' buzzed still. I need to know exactly what's going on to keep all the essence of this shoot together anyways. On top of that, I have to drive back to Tula and don't want to catch a DUI. Those white folks will send a nigga like me back to the penn immediately if I catch another case.

I take UAs every month but I go to GNC to buy a $50 bottle of that Eclipse and drink it about an hour or two before I go see my P.O. Sometimes I have to take a test and sometimes I don't, but I rather be safe than sorry. On top of that, the way I'm runnin' through this bread I'm not trippin' bout no small money.

Hell, I'm thankful for my freedom and that's why I got all these money ventures in the work. I'd rather try and fail then not to try at all. It's a way to make money legally if you really want to make it. The dope/drugs/illegal stuff is just a steppin' stone and a person has to quit that shit eventually because every smooth criminal one day must get caught. It's a proven fact, which is one reason I've been thinkin' bout backin' all the way up from the drug game. I've been havin' dreams of getting setup by homeboys, getting shot, getting locked up and all kinda crazy ass shit.

I've been catchin' lotta envy from dudes round the town because they hate that I'm getting it in by all means necessary. Shit, I been thinkin' bout makin' em hate me even more by going to get me one of those Paul Wall grillz. I know theywill hate to see me with 24 karat gold on top and bottom ice cube blocks with five point diamonds in each one. It will run me prolly ten racks, but it is what it is and it will go with my image.

"Yung Ruff, I really believe in you," Johnny said. "I also enjoy workin' wit' you. I want you to stay focused and not allow the attention or the money gets to you where it begins to control you."

I stand listening to Johnny who looks like he got the Holy Ghost the way he is starin' at me. The look on his face is serious as can be as he places his hand on my shoulder.

"I've worked with lots of artists," he continued. "I've seen some good ones and some not so good ones. What I'm really tryna say is, no matter how good some are, *or aren't*, they lose focus of their goals; their vision. There are many distractors in this game from the women, the money, this, that and if you're not watchful and prayerful, you will fall into it. I might not be makin' sense to you Yung Ruff, but hopefully I am. I don't wanna see you fall into that because it's subtle. I see potential in you that is bigger than what the eye can see."

Johnny nods his head at me and then turns around and walks away.

Thinkin' bout what he was sayin' is crazy because it's always some encounter I have wit' someone off the wall like this and I believe that to be a message from God to me. Of course, I know that it's not true in all circumstances like that.

"Oh well," I say out loud, grabbin' my Swisher Sweet box out my pocket which I got two more blunts already rolled. I grab one out and fire it up. *No time for feelin' guilty Yung Ruff, I* say to myself. I pass the blunt to T who has just walked up. "What up dawg? You enjoyin' yourself?"

"Am I? Dawg, I appreciate you inviting me to the shoot. I remember you was talkin' bout doin' this and to see you doin' it dawg, I'm glad to be a part of it."

"One hunerd. You my dawg and I got you, T. I just wanna see you do good and stay away from the nonsense."

"Got to," T said, passing the blunt back.

We got this last scene and it's time because here comes Johnny and Sam who is my other video editor. Sam is thirty-three, mixed black and white, and is a very good help. He learns a lot from Johnny cause Johnny has a lot more experience. Sam is real cool. He be smokin' bomb with us and all. He doesn't drink or smoke cigarettes, though. He's actually more of the white than the black side of him.

"Time for action! Come on Yung Ruff!" Johnny says. "We have this last scene and then it's over for today. When you drive, only drive about 5 MPH. Sam will be in front of you shooting, and I'll be on the side, so if you're ready, let's get in and go."

"I'm ready," I say, takin' a deep drag of this blunt. "Here you go homie," I say to T, passin' the blunt back to him.

I hop in my Cadillac. I cut the car on and roll down the windows so I can see good. If I didn't roll the windows down, the camera wouldn't be able to see me through my five percent tint. *Block Nigga* is number three on the CD in the deck so I put it on and press Pause.

I'm ready to go, but I'm waiting til' Sam or Johnny signal me.

"Lights, camera, action on three. One. Two. Three. Lights, camera, ACTION!"

I press Play.

I slowly pull off waiting for the next cue so I can start rappin'.

Chapter Twenty-Eight

"Fam," Monkey said immediately as I said hello. "That nigga Loco just got killed. That's what he gets for doing that to JoJo though. It's like the Bible says, *you reap what you sow*," she adds.

That's real talk. Whoever killed em got to em befo' I could. "Where did he get killed at?" I ask.

"I believe it was in Oklahoma City. That's where he went to lay low after he was on the run from down here," she said. "Word is that the police killed him."

"The police!" I exclaimed.

"The police!" she exclaimed.

"I been seein' on the news that these police officers been killin' folks. I mean killin' black folks. Unarmed black folks at that. And the thang about that is they always tryna justify that shit. Now, I wanted that nigga Loco knocked off but for some reason, I hate when police kill niggas. Them pussy ass police need they donuts brought to em," I say.

"You right, Ruff Dawg. Fo' real. I hate how these cops keep killin' niggas, too. We need to start killin' they asses. Fo' real," she said then laughs.

"No bullshit! Well, you know it's goin' down Friday and Saturday at Skinz. I'm gone be performing the new club bangin' single from none other than Yung Ruff, myself. It's called *I Love Women*."

"Fa' sho' FAM. I know it's goin' down. You know Ima be there along with all my goons and goonettes."

"Already. Well, I'm gone get back with you."

I pull up at Kum & Go off of 40th and Okmulgee to get some gas as well as some mango Zig-Zags in the two pack cigarillo package. Coming out the store I see Candy who has pulled up next to me at the gas pump. She got on some black booty shorts that got that thang out there something drastic. I can see her cheeks hangin' out the black cotton booty shorts she wearin'. She gotta know what she doin' out here in the public like this. She got some pretty feet too, that she showin' off in the black flip flops she's wearing.

"Hey Candy!" I say. "How you doin'?"

"Fine," she replies, wavin' at the same time. "I'd be better if you stop playin' hard to get Charles. Stop actin' like you don't want this bomb ass pussy," she jokes playfully while bouncing her ass up and down and looking back at it.

"Ya know Candy, you sho' right. I admit I been trippin' like a muthafucka. I shoulda been done beat that pussy up."

She giggles while blushin' and smilin' at me.

I approach her and give her a hug squeezin' her round ass in which feels like a soft pillow. "What's ya number sexy? I can hook up wit' ya later on after I get from the studio."

"9-1-8-6-1-6-6-1-9-9," she says.

I grab my iPhone 6 and lock her number in immediately.

"I'll see ya later sexy," I say while lickin' my lips and heading back to my 'Lac.

I ride out thinkin' *Woah! What happened right there? I don't give a damn what happened, though, I'm gone fuck the shit outta that girl tonight.* She was lookin' good right there, but I can't wait to see that birthday suit. That's my favorite suit that any woman tryna get my attention can wear to get me all eyes immediately. And right now, Candy is stuck in my mind.

It's still MOB with me which is *money over bullshit*. I know a lotta people say money over *bitches* though. Wit' me it's money over *whatever* is trivial, petty, and undeserving of my attention. Of course, I love pussy, but not more than I love getting these greenbacks. That's why I ain't just been on these fe-lions like that. Besides, these females nowadays are triflin' and unloyal.

Noddin' my head to this 2 Chains.

Walked in then I turn up

In then I turn up

My volume is only on three but the beats are rattlin' the trunk.

Walked in then I turn up

In then I turn up

    I can't help but think how it's already been three months since JoJo got killed. And that Nigga loco was on the run then gets killed by the police. I don't wanna say it like this, but fuck it; if you live by the gun then you die by the gun. Maybe not always, but instill.

    I'm sure Loco's family got a lawsuit on the police for killin' em. I wonder how that nigga got killed and why? Was he tryna fight em, run from em, or what? Word is that he pointed a gun at the police. Suicide-by-cop type of shit. If he did that then the murder is justified and his family ain't getting shit.

Chapter Twenty-Nine

"What's good Candy?" I say as she picks up the phone and says hello in her sexy as can be voice.

"Sittin' here drankin' on this lime twisted gin; waitin' on you," she replied.

"Well, where you live at? I'ma gone head and slide through."

"I'm out here on 6th Street Hill. When you make that first left, then right. I'm right across from the park in the first parking space—apartment 42. You will see my car out there."

"Okay bet baby girl! Ima be through in bout ten minutes."

I hang up the phone thinking, I said baby girl. I'm stupid then a muthafucka for saying that.

I'm fresh out the shower laced with baby powder. I got on my all-red Echo sweat pants and hoodie to match with my black and red Jordans. I had bought me some Grey Goose before the liquor store closed about an hour ago at 9. I got me two packs of 5-pack Swisher Sweets so I am ready to kick it tonight. From what I hear, Candy a super-duper freak, but tonight I'm gone have firsthand experience—not just what others say. Nevermind all them Summit cats bein' in it 'cause tonight it's gone be *me* in it.

I came over my mommas house after I dropped the kids off at they house. I had taken them to watch the new movie, *Fruitopia*. I watched very little of it because I was sleep during most of it.

I turn right on South Side Boulevard coming from Main Street. I'm driving the speed limit because the piggies are out in this area round bout this time. I turn left on 6th Street and go to the stop sign on Kalamazoo Street. I see some young Bloods walkin' from the Hill as I'm headin' up it. I can tell that they are dawgs because of the red flags out their pockets and the bright red shirts.

I take the first left and then first right on 6th Street Hill Apartments. I see Candy's gray 4-door Toyota Camry, just like she said I would. I see a porch light on so I'm assuming that's Candy's light on. I get out my vehicle and start walking toward the apartment. I see #42 lit up on the pole so I know this is Candy's spot.

I ring the doorbell once. Candy comes to the door in her t-shirt and panties and lets me in.

"Hey there sexy!" I say admiring Candy's beauty.

"Hey!" she responds, locking the door back.

"I got some Grey Goose and some of this Sour Diesel Kush if you tryna get wasted."

"Hell yeah," Candy says sittin' down next to me on the leather couch of hers. She starts lickin' on my neck and my ears.

I'm thinkin, *damn, will we even get to drink and smoke? This ol' freaky-ass bitch...*

"Do you know how to roll?" I say.

"Of course I do crazy," she says pushin' my leg in a playful manner.

"Well here sugar. Twist these two blunts up for us."

Reaching into the pockets on my hoodie, I grab the weed and sticks, handing it to her. I grab the Grey Goose and break the seal, taking a good swallow.

"You lookin' good Candy," I say. Her hair is pressed down to her shoulders, no make-up on, skin glowing, and the silk panties she got on got me on hard. I was not expectin' her to be in basically nothing when I came over here. I'm playin' it cool, knowin' really I'm ready to turn her into a pretzel. Instill, I'ma take it slow, which will only make it better.

I take another swallow of this Grey Goose. "Gone drink you some, Candy," I say passing the bottle to her as she grabs it wit' one hand. Using her other hand she finishes lickin' one of the blunts and hands it to me. I light it up.

The slow jams playin' in the background are very soothing. Marques Houston, *Naked*, is coming through the speakers, which I've always loved this song.

Come on, baby, turn the lights off, lets get naked (Ooh, come on)

Come on, baby girl, you know I just can't take it.

(I can't take it no more)

Let your panties hit the floor, (floor)

Let your body steal the show right now (Right now)

It seems like you're ready, so come on girl,

I just can't wait to see us naked... (us naked, yeah)

Candy truly is a freak and I see now she got a porno playin' on TV with the volume down. Ain't no way a nigga can resist lookin' at it. Pinky got that thang tooted up and her fat ass pussy getting banged from behind, doggy style. She is lookin' back at the camera man makin' those fuck-faces. I'm just statin', not complaining, because I loves to get freaky myself.

I pass the blunt to Candy who passes me back the bottle. I take another deep swallow, then one more. The way I drink, instead of sipping, it never takes me long to get lit.

"Here, Candy, you can finish this bottle off," I say.

My hand is on her pussy and using my fingers I'm massagin' it. I can feel her pussy through these silk panties and its *wet!* I know she likes it because she opened her legs wider as I'm feelin' on it. I can feel her grindin' on my fingers as well. I hit the blunt one more good time and place it in the ashtray. Candy just finished knockin' off the Grey Goose and I know she's buzzed 'cause I'm good.

I get on my knees in front of her. Slowly I start pulling off her panties as she helps by putting her legs up in the air. Her fat ass pussy is looking edible as I dive in face first and start by licking on her pearl tongue. Candy has her hands on my head applying pressure. I like the fact that she is doing that too, because it lets me know that she wants it.

I swear that she got the prettiest pussy ever. On top she gots the sweetest juices I've ever tasted. I got my hands on her hamhocks, pushin' them to help keep her legs elevated. I'm suckin' on her pussy lips and they are very delicious. For Candy to be twenty-eight years old, she still got pussy lips like a virgin. Most women her age be havin' shredded or potted meat looking pussy.

Seeing how tight this thang is I wonder if it's true bout her being a hoe. Or better yet, a promiscuous woman who done been ran through. I'm lickin' from the pearl all the way down to her ass with no shame. Listening to her moans and groans makes me lick even harder. I can feel her grinding her pussy and palpitating it on my face. Her hands are in my head, her fingernails grasped in my braids. My tongue is spellin' out C-A-N-D-Y on her pearl tongue, over and over…

Candy's body is shiverin' and shakin' as she squirts cum out her pussy. I suck it all up, makin' sure I swallow all of her candy. As I continue suckin' on her pussy, she pushes my head away. I never have seen a squirter like this. *Damn!*

"It tickles. Back up," she says.

I keep on goin' for a lil' bit just to let her know I'm in control.

I get up and kick my shoes off, followed by my sweatpants and boxers. Standing at attention in front of Candy, she grabs my dick and starts suckin' on it like a professional. I can tell that she has her DSL's, which is abbreviation for *Dick Suckin' License.*

While she suckin' on my dick and balls, I take off my sweat shirt and put both my hands on her head as she greedily devours my package. Her eyes continuously lookin' at me in intense passion and delight.

"Suck this ma'fucka like you never sucked dick befo' girl," I say. My knees beginning to buckle and my toes beginning to curl. I can feel that I'm about to bust all in her mouth. "I'm bout to bust," I say but Candy continues to suck on my dick so I bust all inside her mouth. It feels good as she makes sure she sucks all the nut out of my dick hole.

Candy lies down on the couch with her pussy purred up at me. I follow suit and get on the couch with her. One leg I have on the couch and the other leg is on the floor. I got her legs up in the air, pressing her knees to her face. I was about to go up in her but say, "Hold on, let me grab a rubber." I grab the Trojan condom out of my sweat pants pocket. I open the wrapper and squeeze the rubber around my dick.

"I'm ready to beat yo' pussy up now girl."

I resume my position on top of Candy who is passionately waiting. I stick my dick inside her slow and gentle. Candy's tight pussy feels so good as I go in and out of her. Her pussy is like a glove cause it's grabbing on to my dick like a vaccum. I'm willin' to bet that she has one of the tightest pussies in the world for her age.

I speed up faster and faster, knockin' her head up and down on the arm of the couch. She places one hand against the couch to stop her head from hitting it. With her other hand she has on my lower stomach. Her eyes are closed as she is in ecstasy, biting on her lips and moaning out, "Charles…Charles…"

All I'm thinking is *beat the life out this bitch's pussy!*

I'm feeling a nut coming on so I continue going hard until I bust. Taking my dick out her pussy I notice that the condom busted. *Fuck it*, I say.

"The condom busted, Candy."

"It's okay. I'm on birth control, anyway."

"Oh. Well, stand up and bend over the arm of this couch as I beat yo' pussy doggystyle from the back."

Candy gets up and does exactly like told.

I waste no time getting up behind her putting my dick deep inside her pussy. Her fat ass booty is bouncin' on me, violently. I stand and let her work it as I hold onto her waist and she backs her pussy all on me.

The warmth of her vagina is so delightful. I feel her pussy walls vice-gripped to my dick, or so it seems. Candy is bouncin' her ass on me so hard that I have to brace the couch. I'm holdin' on though. Just watchin' her is a pleasure. My dick hard as a rock, my butt cheeks squeezed tight, and my eyes closed. I gasp as I cum all up in Candy's pussy. I'm steady pumpin' away at her now.

"Take this dick! All of it!" It's like I got a boost of energy or second wind. "Go ahead and lay back on the couch sexy," I say to Candy who immediately jumps up and does exactly like I told her to do. I love it when a woman knows how to listen.

"Yes daddy," she says. She lies on the couch and begins fingering her pussy. Now she's lickin' and suckin' all on her fingers.

Yeah, I gotta super-duper freak on my hands. Ol' nasty ass bitch, I say to myself.

I grab Candy's legs and stuff em into the couch as I put my dick back into her pussy and begin stroking. I got her head all squashed in the couch. She is moanin' and groanin'. My dick is giving her pussy a swellin' how I'm hammering in and outta her at max speed. I'm tryna put my dick in her stomach and I know it is from the way she's squirming. I feel like I done took an X pill, smoked some Wet or took a Viagra or somethin' now. I continue pounding away for over an hour until I bust a nut up in her again.

I get up and stretch. Candy continues to lay there. She rolls over and goes to sleep. I can see daylight out the window so I wipe myself off in the restroom and put back on my clothes. I grab the blunts off the table that Candy rolled up but we never did get to finish 'em. As I head out the door I look at Candy's fat ass one mo' time then leave out.

Fucked that bitch to sleep, I chuckle to myself.

Chapter Thirty

I dedicate this song to JoJo.
JoJo, it's so sad you had to go, but I know
You're up in heaven lookin' down on me, bro.
In memory of your name, I call this song JoJo....

The club was jumpin', as usual, when I got up to perform. I had to rep it for JoJo. The streets are still talkin' about how Loco got killed by the police while on the run for murdering JoJo. Matter fact, word is that Loco's momma got a big wrongful death lawsuit against the Oklahoma City Police department. His momma is still fighting for the civil suit, but she will win most likely. Come to find out Loco didn't point a gun at the police. From what everybody says, Loco was running from the police with his hands up when the police fired two shots. One hit him in the head and the other bullet hit his neck. To everyone's surprise, he didn't have a gun on him though. He's another unarmed black man killed by punk ass police.

Sitting here in the VIP with J3, I fire up this L while thinkin' heavy. "Bro, you know we gone have to slow down. Well, actually, *stop* all this wild living we doing. I know we making lots of money and we are having lots of fun but we are living wordly, not Godly."

"Yeah I know bro," J3 says. "I actually have been thinkin' bout the same thing. I'm tired of lookin' over my shoulders from selling these drugs. God knows we ain't tryna be getting popped but we know that we can't keep on with this stuff because it has a date to it. An expiration date."

These strippers in here are lookin' good slidin' up and down the poles and walkin' round deliverin' drinks. In the back room we got tricks payin' big money for our strippers. This escort service is making lots of money for me and J3. It's actually making more than this club is, even though they are hooked in together.

Me and J3 have always been close since kids. Our daddy use to always tell us to fight *with*, not against each other. I was the bad one out of both of us. J3 was a good kid compared to me. J3 had hands on him, though. I remember when we were in Coweta living and bro fought this one chink dude and gave him the business. Another time in Country Village Apartments I had got into it with Prestle, the all-state wrestling champion. I fought him then J3 did. I didn't do nothin' compared to how J3 demolished him.

I've never been real big on fighting, even though I never did back down from any fights, either. From the days of my youth, a lot of things have changed. When I look back, I'm thankful that God has kept me in His loving arms and care.

I still have my struggles, but I'm steady pushing forward. I'm glad that I am not locked up and that I still have breath which is a blessing in itself. I'm ready for this divorce to be through with my wife. Monday we finally go to court to get it finalized. I hate callin' Nelle my wife because she is a big dumby. She steady chasin' dick like its money. She done got kicked out her house because of her little eighteen year old boyfriend, Scrappy.

I know that we live and we learn but what she is doing makes no sense. It's like, *damn woman; didn't I teach you anything about these no good ass niggas?* I swear, she had to have went to school to get a 'stupid bitch' degree. I bet she got a 4.0 grade average at that shit, too.

"Look at her stupid ass on the dance floor, J3."

"Fuck her," J3 says. "These bitches gone do what they want to so let em do it. It don't matter how good you be to em, they still ain't loyal. Take care of yo' kids like *I* do and don't even trip off that hoe. I know she ya wife and you love her, but bro, I wouldn't give her no time. If you do, somethin' wrong wit' you."

"I'm knowin', J3. It's just crazy that this is the one I vowed to love. But hey, it is what it is. I gots to move on. 2 Sweet got popped by the Feds a couple days ago. Word on the street is that he gave up my name and a few other peddlers he had. It's hard to believe that he would turn snitch, but in this game you never do know. Pressure does make diamonds but it also *busts pipes, I do know for sure,* I thought.

"We gone change some stuff up," J3 said. "Just in case we are under surveillance by the Feds. I mean it's not like we ain't got money stacked up already and the club is jumpin'. But I'm the same way as you on 2 Sweet. I highly doubt he would turn snitch. But I do believe that they are definitely tryna get him to. We gotta stay on our Ps and Qs bro."

Chapter Thirty-One

I'm Sittin' in this courtroom, waitin' on the judge to come back in from a ten minute recess. All the paperwork is filed for the divorce. We will have joint custody over our two kids. She keeps everything that belongs to her and I keep everything that belongs to me.

I'm thankful that this long process is finally about to be over for good. This divorce has been up and down for the last two years and, boy or boy, I'm happy it's finished.

Obviously, I loved this woman, or I wouldn't have married her. The thang about that is, the woman I met ten years ago, she is not the same. It reminds me of an R&B song I wrote called, 'What *Happened To Love'*, which is about us.

We used to be down like Bonnie and Clyde.
Now, it's like we're strangers cause we don't even say Hi.
Why? What happened to Love?

That's the question that I ask, when I think about us…

The answer is—she changed. She kicked me out her life when she found another lover/man. I remember she told me that this dude swept her off her feet. She thought he was Mr. Prince Charming. All I can say is this woman is gullable and naïve. She is falling for Muskogee niggas and she always talkin' bout, *ain't nobody worried bout these Muskogee niggas,* but it's obvious to see that she is.

She is sittin' in the front of the courtroom lookin' all innocent, knowin' she is guilty than a mug. Her hair is in a ponytail and she is wearing her glasses today, instead of contacts. The white shirt she is wearing reads *Women Rock* in multiple bold colors. A pair of Capri pants she wears with some white and pink Nike Shox. She keep lookin' in my direction but she doin' it on the sly, tryna act like she ain't.

In my mind I'm thinkin', *Yeah bitch, it's over now.* I ain't cut her since before I went to jail last time so I know them miles are way up there.

"All rise," the bailiff says as the judge comes back from break.

"In the case between Charles Ruffin versus Nelle Ruffin…"

"Yes your Honor. We have everything ready and all we need is your signature to finalize this divorce," I said.

"Do you oppose, Mrs. Ruffin?"

"No, Sir, your Honor," she said.

The judge reads over the divorce agreement, signs it and says, "As of now, the two of you are now legally divorced. Next case."

"Nelle," I say out loud; louder than I intended as we walked out of the courtroom. "I need to talk to you on a serious note."

She turns around and places her hand on her hip while pooching out her lips. "Yeah?"

"Let's go outside and get outta this courthouse," I said in a nonchalant type of way.

I can't help but look at her ass as she is walkin' in front of me. I admit I do gotta problem with lookin' at fat booties. I mean, Nelle is actually skinny, but with these Capri's she got on, *Shawty rockin' that shit!*

"On a serious note, Nelle, I want the best for you. I know that we haven't been seeing eye to eye but we gone have to get along, at least for the kids' sake. Matter fact, I got ten thousand that I'm giving to you to spend on the kids, as well as yourself, to help out a little bit. I'm not giving you this money for nothing in return. Like I've told you many of times, I will always love you and want what's best for you. I will be more than happy to come get the kids this weekend. I will be down from Tulsa around one PM on Saturday. Follow me to my truck and I will give you the money."

"Charles, I hope one day you will find it in your heart to forgive me because I'm truly sorry and I still love you, although I rarely admit it," Nelle says.

"It's all good, shawty. No sweat, besides, everything happens for a reason."

"I like this truck you got. It's 2016 too," she says.

"Yeah, I appreciate it. I bought it last week. All black just like I like it, four-door Silverado," I say while reaching in the glove compartment and grabbing two envelopes containing five racks each. "Here you go, Nelle."

"Thank you, Charles."

"You welcome Nelle," I say, giving her a hug at the same time. "I will get back with you, Nelle. Take care."

I hop in my truck, close the door and start the engine. I shake my head, lookin' at Nelle while she walkin' to get in her car. I really still can't believe how she dogged me out like she did when I was gone. I know I need to get over it but its hard, especially because I took her back when I was in and she still did me in again. Some females just ain't got any sense.

"Life goes on," I say out loud as I exit the courthouse parking lot.

\

Chapter Thirty-Two

"OPEN THE DOOR! OPEN THE DOOR! It's the UNITED STATES MARSHALS! OPEN THE FUCKIN' DOOR!!!"

Boom! Boom! Boom!

As I wake up from this deep sleep I hear beating on the door and screaming. I immediately know what time it is.

"Ain't this 'bout a bitch," I said as the door is kicked off the hinges.

"Get down on the floor, RIGHT NOW! Put your hands on top of your head! We have a warrant for your arrest, Yung Ruff—AKA Charles Ruffin—for conspiracy. We've been watching you for the past year and a half, since the last time you got out. It wasn't you we were after. It was 2 Sweet whom we've been watching the last five years. But just like any game, it's a sequence of operation. Whenever we are watching one drug dealer, then we will always encounter *more* drug dealers."

This is some bullshit, I'm thinkin' to myself. I knew this game whatn't nothin' but a shame. Instill, I hopped back in it, hopin' for it to be different this time and only deceived myself. Headed out the door and into the patrol car, I can't help but think how I let myself down and my kids down—*once again.*

The one person I let down the most was God and I know I have got to pay the price for my behavior in which I know is wrong.

It seems to be a hundred carloads of police. The whole block is filled with Feds and DEA. I'm sittin' here lookin' at these laws through the backseat of this police vehicle thinkin' to myself, *here we go again...*

I knew I could,'t keep on sellin' drugs and get away with it forever. I was planning on stopping, but it seems once I started was the biggest mistake ever. When the police said that they had been watching 2 Sweet for the last five years it let me know that 2 Sweet did not snitch but they had him under surveillance so long that I got caught up in the middle of his hot pursuit in which they were already on him.

There's nothing in my house as far as drugs are concerned. I don't have any guns either, so if the conspiracy is all they have on me, then that should be it.

Ain't no need to cry, now, I tell myself as the police drive off, taking me to the Muskogee County Jail in which holds federal inmates for the North Eastern District. I'm no stranger to this ride or this feeling, but this time it's worse than before. I've heard people say, *if I ever get locked up again, I'm goin' Fed. Go Big or Go Home* they say.

Well, I've never said that and I see that I should have stayed home, cause now I'm in some shit that I don't know how I'm gone wiggle free from. Entering into this county jail has got me feeling sick to my stomach already. My anxiety is kickin' my ass and I feel like I can barely even *breathe.*

I'm thinkin' bout all that's done happened in the last year and a half. It took me no time to get sucked back in the game. I really deceived myself thinking that I would never get caught up again when I'm doin' the same stuff that has gotten many people locked up for long times at a time. *This* time it's *really* an eye-opener, because the shit has definitely hit the fan. My mind is racing like a rat trying to avoid a cat.

Every OG or old schooler in the game that I know done said, "The game ain't the same now as it was back in the day."

Right now I feel just like my old school potna, Cheese. Cheese is from Haskell, Oklahoma. I met him last time I was in jail. It was in 2012 as a matter fact. He was tall, around 6' 2". He kept his hair balled or the rest of it balled to fit his already balled top head. He would say, "Ruff, I ain't jailhouse material!"

I knew I was wrong, but on the other hand, I whatn't hurtin' nobody. I mean, nothing that they were not tryna indulge theirself in. One thang I ain't doin' is turning snitch, so they just gone have to do what they gone do. I'm hopin' someday I can get up outta this! I got the money this time to pay for the best lawyer. I do know from experience through other ballers that with these Feds you can't buy them with money like you can buy a case in the state court.

The same procedure as always when you're in jail. This time they sent me upstairs, right away, to Cell Block 9 where the Federal inmates are kept. I didn't see anybody I knew right off top so I put my mat on the rack. Luckily I ain't got no celly right now. I'm just in here thinkin', what *is my next move?* And also, *what is my BEST move?*

One thing I do know is I'm not tryna be movin' too fast. This Fed stuff is a process. I know they have a high conviction rate. Now, they can be beat, but it all depends and that's still slim to none. In other words, it's *very* hard.

Things were jumpin' for me. Now I got this log in the road.

I know my kids gone be mad at me. Both of em.

Lil' Charles and Charliah, I told them Daddy wasn't gone *ever* get locked up again. Now they gone think I lied to em. And the thing about that is I didn't *mean* to lie to em. I didn't *want* to come back to this hell hole.

I guess I made a promise based on wishful thinkin'. I can relate to the jailbirds who make promises or make vain speech like that. We really do be serious when we say what we say, at least *eight* times outta ten, we do. In this game it's crazy, but we know there are consequences. The smartest thang is to *not be in the game*. Go right all the way, and don't play with fire and then expect not to get burnt. If it's a chance that you can get locked up for something then it's not worth the risk of losin' your freedom because Murphy's Law is real.

I know there has to be somethin' that I can do. *Somethin'*. At least, that's what I'm tellin' myself.

This is some bullshit.

It was a long ride from Tulsa at my house to this Muskogee County Jail. It's now worser than ever at this jail, I can already feel it. Besides that, I'm no rookie at this. I remember my first merry-go-round at fifteen years old. It seems to stand true that every time that I came after that, it has been *worse*. I'm speakin' from the feeding on down to the inch of everything else in this raggedy jail that needs refurbished.

I know one thing for sure is this: I'm gone *truly* get myself together. I'm not gone get back out *this* time and sell drugs—*at all*. Because I can see that I did not need to after I got on my feet, I know I should've been done stopped completely, cause the money started lookin' straight on my end. I did have some legal businesses jumpin' off but it still did no good when I was still playin' Mr. Dope Man in which is why I'm layin' here in this jail cell.

I can't believe I'm in this zoo *again*. I mean, ain't no way I was *tryna* be in this zoo again. I know that this is no dream. Its reality and I have to face this trial the best way I know how and that's to remain silent, keep my head up, and stay prayed up. Also, I have to keep in mind that I came in this *bitch* alone and I'm gone leave this *bitch* alone.

"Stop running from your calling Charles!" I hear a voice say.

The power from the voice pushed me off my king-size bed on to the floor in which I woke up drenching in sweat from head to toe like I took a shower and didn't dry off. My head is pounding fast. Not knowing what's going on, I thank God for another day. I lift my hands up and praise Him for keeping me safe and out of lockup or, even worse, killed running these Oklahoma streets chasing after a piece of paper.

"I can't *do* this no more!" I scream out loud. "I can't do this no more! I'm tired of this. I'm through. I'm *through*! I give it all up. It's not worth it no more. *I'm through!*"

I realize now that I have got to change and live a cross life instead of a Ruff Lyfe. This Ruff Lyfe thug-livin' ain't worth me being away from my kids again. I done gave this game my all and in return this game is still the same—*nothin' but a shame.*

Warning comes before destruction and this nightmare, I'm gone call it, has opened my eyes wide. My middle finger is to this game. It's a battlefield of the mind, and mind is the master. If I continue to fall weak, then I will continue to be weak, but if I start standing strong, then that's when I will be strengthened.

I'm blessed that I did not get popped by the Feds. God knows it's plenty times I've been paranoid, waiting on the kick door. Especially after my boy 2 Sweet got popped. The streets were talkin' big on how he gave me up and for a minute I didn't know, but then again I knew 2 Sweet is a solid ass nigga from way back. I get up heading directly for the shower to get all this sweat off me from this eye-opening dream that still got me like, *dang!*

My heart is still pounding and my mind still racing.

I'm glad it was only a dream.

Chapter Thirty-Three

Since I've been shooting videos and keeping them on *YouTube* and *Vevo*, my following has increased dramatically. My music is on every available social networking site for artists including *Sound Cloud, Reverbnation, Instagram* and *Facebook,* just to name a few. All digital stores have Ruff Lyfe music as well.

It's January 2017, and it's finally the time for my double mixtape to drop Friday; Ruff Lyfe, *Still No Features.* Some say that I shouldn't give away so much music at one time like this, but what I say is it ain't trickin' if you got it. I don't need no features on my mixtape either, so *forget* these critics. I've learned already, and I always keep in mind that wherever there is opportunity, there is also opposition.

J-Serious has done lots of promotion work for me behind the scenes. I'm very pleased with the work that has been done. Friday, at Skinz, I'm gone perform two songs live off of the mixtape. *On the Strength* and *Rubbin' On You* have been getting' major airplay and are favorites of the fans. I love the fans and I am dedicated to giving them the music that they want to hear and nothing less.

When I was younger I thought it was harder than this to get in the industry, but for me it's been smooth sailing now that I have fully put all my energy and strength into rapping. I've made a conscious decision that I'm not selling any more drugs. I'm going 100% legal from this point on. Besides, with 2 Sweet on lock, now I *know* I have to stay cool. It's not like I'm making a lot of money with this rapping but I just do it cause it's what I love.

Of course, I'm *still* connected in the game. I had been coppin' thru this Mexican from Southside Locos in OKC named Essay. It's been all love and dirt cheap prices, but it's over with. Besides, the game is not to be stuck in anyways. You have to get in and get out.

J-Serious told me that some record companies have been calling asking about me but right now I don't want to make the wrong decision. I hear so much about signing to major labels that ain't good. It got me on ten toes, but don't' get me wrong, I just might accept the recording contract from *Capitol Records*.

I remember when I was around 11 or 12 and we were in Hollywood on Sunset Boulevard walkin' the stars. I had seen *Capitol Records* and wanted to go inside so my brother-in-law Fedro and my sister Sandra took me inside the building. Of course I didn't see any major artists because they're not usually in the lobby and can't just anybody see them. It was a black lady receptionist who was nice and realized that I was just a curious kid interested in music. She told me that I couldn't go up the elevators which was were all the artists, managers, and producers were. I was just so happy to be there that I asked her if I could take a picture with her and she happily agreed. Now I'm really recording music and I have the opportunity to do what I've always wanted to do and it's truly a humbling experience.

I checked the other day on my *YouTube* and my views have been climbing. It's crazy cause with social media, I'm connected with people all over the world. With the internet it's too easy to make this money off your music with digital distribution.

I'm thinkin' bout all types of legal ways to get this money right now. I ain't gotta sell drugs ever again. I feel like as long as you got the determination and willpower there's nothing you can't do. Well obviously, you should keep God first, no matter what you do.

Chapter Thirty-Four

Bottles on me, I supply on the Strength.

Drugs on me, I supply on the Strength.

Whatever you need, I supply on the Strength.

Well, I'm tryna get the coochie, ain't gone lie on the Strength...

The club is packed like sardines tonight. We like Mexicans piled up in this mug. It's all love, though, and I'm feelin' ecstatic tonight. I just finished performing on stage and the crowd was showin Ruff Lyfe super-duper love.

I've got so many positive remarks on the mixtape that I'm excited. It's my first time ever to have a CD in the stores. All of the writing I done in the penitentiary payed off. When I got out, I had over 350 songs to play with so I was well ahead of the game.

J3 set this bitch right in here tonight. It's usually left to him for the lighting and decorations or any special effects on the dance floor. He even came up with the idea that tonight was drinks free. The charge at the door is $10 a pop though. Also, he had advised me to give everyone a mixtape before they leave the club tonight.

Of course, I will have bouncers take care of it, but at first I said *Hell naw'll. I ain't givin' all those away for FREE!* But it actually makes perfect sense. I just want people to feel it, which I know they will, which increases my fan base. You do the math, lookin' at how crowded it is in here. Times that by ten and we are talkin' *ching...ching.*

"What up Poopie," I say as he stumbles pass me with two females on his arms, cheesin'. Poopie always was the type a guy who be pullin' them women. I think he be trickin' on em, but hey, whatever to get the coochie. It is what it is. *On the strength*, like the song says. I mean, he be givin' em the drugs or whatever they want. Now days these females is some drug addicts and if you can feed that habit, then you gone get some additives.

I got one more song to perform before the night is over so I'm just lookin' it in with J3 right here at my side and we drinkin' on some Incredible Hulk—*Hennessey* and *Hypnotic*. Since I decided that it's no more drugs selling, J3 has been locked in with me. Matter fact, he has his own trucking company called New Level Trucking. J3 really ain't ever been with the nonsense like I have. All he has been in the game for is the money because he takes *good* care of his four kids. I'm very proud of J3 and not just because he is my brother, but in all truth, he is a leader and a role model.

I already told my whole crew that it's over with for sellin'.

T, B Moore, Notch, Monkey, C Nutz, C 4, Braze and Shot G are a few of my guys in Skinz now. They are all here to support my mixtape and on top of that, Skinz is just the place to be. It doesn't matter if you male or female at Skinz, there is a treat for you.

I'm tipsy than a mug tonight, already. I just finished the cup of Incredible Hulk and now I'm listening to this music and waiting for my next performance which is coming very soon. Everybody who is somebody is here tonight. From the lil' chicks that I done knocked off recently to the ones back in the days. I mean, I ain't tryna brag, but the mixtape goes hard. On top of that, I'm no rookie to Muskogee and I got mad love in this town. Even though I'm not living here no more, it's still nothing but love.

"Ladies and gentlemen, we have another performance from none other than Yung Ruff," the DJ says as everyone goes wild, clapping, whooping, and hollerin' *Yung Ruff, Yung Ruff.* I have to admit it feels good to be shown this much love. I grab the mic from the DJ and the beat drops as I'm noddin' my head and in tune with the beat.

Rubbin' on you, touchin' on you.

Kissin' on you, lovin' on you.

Doin' all them things that them love birds do.

Everytime I'm wit' you I be rubbin' on you...

Rubbin' on you, touchin' on you.

Kissin' on you, lovin' on you.

Doin' all them things that them love birds do.

Everytime I'm wit' you, I be rubbin' on you...

Exotic ya body, the way you move, so naughty.

You show-stoppin' the party, when you up in the party.

We got the liquor Bacardi, Hennessey and the Goose.

We got whatever, name a price Shawty, I give it to you.

I wanna see you get loose, girl gone and do what you do.

Gone and hang out wit' cha crew, if that's what you wanna do.

You wanna be independent, always handle ya business.

Always dressed to impress, head ta toe, you be fresh.

I enjoy being on the stage and doing this music but I would be a liar if I didn't say that I've gained more haters than I've ever had in my life. I mean, when you getting money like *I'm* getting and you getting the ladies, too.

These niggas hate hella hard because they women want the Yung Ruff.

Out of everybody that's in the club tonight, it's only one person I ain't seen yet—and I'm actually shocked about it—Nelle. Nelle knows it's poppin' tonight and usually has her momma or daddy watch the kids so that she could go out but not this night which seems very strange to me. I know I can't stand that woman, but it's obvious I still love her and try not to but it's hard not to think about her. I just knew out of everybody, she would have been here to support me.

My sisters are here, even though they don't do the clubbin' like that. They decided to come just because tonight it's the celebration of my CD being in stores.

I can't help but to notice Mini lookin' extra sexy tonight like a diva with that jean skirt on, plain black shirt, and some all-black flats. I have not hit Mini since about 3 month after we first met, but looking at her got me hard as a rock right now. I wouldn't mind making it spark like Independence Day with her but word around town is she mess with Tommy Shaw, which is that cat who was with Loco that night when JoJo got killed. I don't fuck with that nigga like that but that's another story.

I'm still pissed off about how the situation turned out. It is what it is, though, I have to admit. Besides that, I ain't fronted her no work or Monkey in over four or five months. I had to cut them off because Monkey called me talkin' bout someone stole a Chevy from her at her house. A Chevy ain't that much, but hey that's two and a quarter ounces of powder cocaine. I told her don't worry bout it and ain't messed with neither one of them since on that type of tip.

I didn't buy that bullshit ass story that they tried to sell me. Even if it *was* true, ain't no way Monkey should be havin' all those niggas and hoes over her house all the time and steady runnin' her mouth. I don't give a damn, family or not, when you fuck up then you cut off and that's what happened with them.

I know Mini had nothing to do with that but instill, she started slow playing on payments so since I cut off Monkey and I met Mini though Monkey, they both got the boot. I will always look out for Monkey, though, because she family. But we can't do business.

The smell of pussy is all through this club. It smells like a thousand pussies are spread open and a huge fan is blowing it through the ductwork in this building. Its women running around in here ass-naked giving up the coochie left and right. For the most part, everyone goes to the backroom and pays a fee, but just like any place of business, some people break the rules.

I walk from the VIP to the bar where two women are starting up a commotion. One looks familiar to me and it is Monkey trippin' wit' some chick. It sounds like she is trippin' about someone messing with her husband. The thang about that is that they're separated so Monkey needs to leave that alone and move on. I'm sittin' here deciding *should I stop it?* The other girl, to my surprise, is Candy.

"Y'all break this shit up," I say. "If y'all got a problem with each other, handle that shit somewhere else, not in my club or in my parking lot."

Monkey swings a wild punch over the top of me and clocks Candy in her nose. By this time, security is thick over here at the bar.

"Go ahead and kick em out the club," the big 6 foot 5 black bouncer said to the other three. "Let one go and then the other go about fifteen minutes later."

Security escorts Candy out first, whose nose is bleeding at this time because Monkey got her pretty good.

Security takes Monkey to the Red Room, which is the room where people got to chill out before we kick em out.

Now that that ruckus is over, I grab me one more drink of Incredible Hulk. I've been drinkin' it all night so ain't no need to change up. The music is still jumping and the dance floor is doing the same thang. Some people are playing pool on the tables while some are backed in, posted up on the walls. Others are in the back rooms getting sexual favors.

People are doin what they do and it's all good as long as they're not fighting or acting foolish in here. Foolishness I can't have, because no matter what people may think, this club Skinz is a business and will be run in that manner. Fights break out in clubs, of course, but they're still not tolerated.

I head over to VIP where I see J3 entertained by three dollar pieces. I can't even call em dimes cause it would be disrespect.

"What up J3? What up ladies?" I say in an awe spoken tone.

"I'm just choppin' it up with these sexy models from out of town. They're from Texas and heard about our club and wanted to check us out because they've been hearing how hard it jumps."

"Oh yeah, it jumps like jumpin' jacks," I say with a smile, lookin' at these ladies with persuasion on my face. All three of these sexy ladies smile at me and blush. "By the way, I'm Yung Ruff." I stick my hand out to shake their hands, kissing it as I shake their hand.

All three of these yellow bones are bad. They so bad that I got a boner right now, talkin' to em. All three of em look like they are Dominican or Rihanna's kinfolk and that's a good thang. As long as I have wanted to hit

Rihanna, these chicks will take her place. *I'm gone have to hit one of these ladies,* I say to myself while lickin' my lips and lookin' them up from head to toe.

"I see you, Yung Ruff," J3 says. "Gone and have fun with em if you want, bro. Their all yours if you want."

"Aiight, bet. Y'all ladies comin' wit' me," I say as I head to the backroom. All three of em are behind me and I'm knowin' sparks gone fly back here.

In the backrooms it's live. I done had many, *many,* sexy thangs in this area. I gotta lil' sayin' about the backroom that goes like this: *What goes on back here stays back here.*

I hear the ladies gigglin' as I open the door and one by one they giddy on in. I slap the last one on her backside in adoration. She looks back at me and smiles. *Oh, hell yeah!* I'm thinkin' as I close the door and lock it.

Oops. I Almost forgot to grab the 'Occupied' sign to hang on the door.

I grab the sign off the wall that's hangin' up right next to the door. I unlock the door and open it back up and hang the occupied sign up on the door.

Same process again, I close the door and lock it behind me.

I turn to the ladies who are over there kissin' and lickin' on each other. Ima have some fun tonight. I'm already feelin' good from the dranks that I put in my system. I'm actually feelin' like my drink was spiked cause I actually feel like I done took a X pill. Right now I ain't trippin' cause I'm tryna fuck like I'm on an X pill.

The music is jammin' from the stereo that's playin' Ginuwine's album *Differences*; or whatever it's called. I take off my black and gray Nike Air Max shoes. I take off my all-black Red Monkey jeans. I'm lookin' at the ladies who have already got their clothes off. One is eatin' one pussy and that one is eatin' the other one's pussy.

I go up to the one who is getting' her pussies ate and pull down my boxers and stick my dick in her wet mouth as she begins suckin' my eyeballs into the back of my head. This bitch is dynamite. She ain't shit to be played with.

All the moanin' in this mug lets me know this is how it goes down when you'se a celebrity and that's *definitely* what I am now. I mean, I ain't tryin' to, but then again, I *gotta* show out like I'm doin' now.

My knees want to give in how she is suckin' on my dick. Her head is goin' super-duper fast then super slow. She is lickin' it from top to bottom. She puts her whole mouth back over my dick. She uses her hand, jackin' my dick off and suckin' on it at the same time. My hands on her hair which she has whipped up from the beauty shop, it looks.

. I begin to shiver and I know that I'ma bout to bust a nut all in her mouth. My dick is harder than steel as she speeds up her motor mouth and I bust one in her mouth. Then two and then three. My nut is squirtung out as I let out a deep breath in relief. It's like I was underwater, drownin' and needed air, then finally got oxygen. She is steady suckin' on my dick and makin' sure she slurps every drip-drop. My dick is tingling so I take it out her mouth.

I go to the other girls. The one that's eatin' the other one's pussy has her pussy all up in the air. I get behind her and look at her fat ass and pretty pussy. I squeze my dick into her tight pussy in which feels like some virgin pussy, although I know ain't Nan one of these freaks no virgins.

As long as it feels like it I'm cool, though.

Her warm tight pussy, I'm going deep in as I listen to her moan while eatin' the other girl's pussy. I continue strokin' in and out of her pussy. I pull my dick out right before I bust and shoot cum all over her ass cheeks and back.

My phone rings so I go grab it out of my pants pockets. It's 3:30 in the morning and it's Nelle's mother. I answer the phone and Debbie, Nelle's mother, is screaming.

"I can't understand you," I say. "Now what is it?"

"It's Nelle! She overdosed on some pills and is in the Muskogee hospital right now!"

"I'll be there ASAP," I assure her. "I'm about to leave the club now."

"Okay," she says as I press end.

"I gotta go," I say to the ladies who are still freaked out over there. "I gotta go! Put on y'all fucking clothes. It's time to get up outta here," I say.

I put back on my clothes, thinking, *what the hell really done went on with Nelle? Where the kids at? Is Nelle gone be okay?*

The club is empty now as I head out and lock up the building.

"It was nice to meet you ladies," I say as they head to their all-grey Tahoe that they came in.

I hop in my truck and head out to go to Muskogee hospital.

Chapter Thirty-Five

I sped from the club as quickly as I could, thankful that I did not receive a ticket by any police on the way. As I enter the hospital I see Nelle's family standing around crying.

"She gone! She gone! My baby is gone!" Debbie is cryin'. I give her a hug and comfort her just by holding on to her.

I see my kids sitting in the chair by the window. They run to me when they see me, as well.

"Daddy! Mamma died."

"It's gone be okay," I say holding both of them in my arms as they shed tears. "I got y'all, Charles and Charliah. I'm gone raise y'all the way I'm supposed to, as well. I love y'all."

"We love you too," both of them say.

"Where is Nelle at right now?" I ask her dad, Toby.

"She's still back there as of what we know from the doctor who just came in about ten minutes earlier. The doctor told us that they did all that they can do and it was nothing else that they could do."

So much is on my mind right now. I'm in complete shock about all this right now. I wonder if it's something else I could've done or should've done that could've prevented Nelle from overdosin' on Xanax bars. The fact that life is short really hits home now. Out of all the stuff me and Nelle been through, never once did I want her to die. I never thought the last time we seen each other would be the last.

Why, God? I say, "I know you are in control, but this is hard and we all need your comfort right now, in Jesus' name.

When I didn't see Nelle at Skinz last night I should've called and checked on her. I mean, I figured she was just chillin' and doin' what she does. Nelle always wanted her independence and did not want anyone up on her. But if she wanted something, she would go get it. She went the extra mile for me for several years and I know that she will do it for any man that got her heart. She will stay loyal to that man and this I know because we were, at one time, Ace Boon Coon, Bonnie and Clyde, lovers and friends. Nelle was my everything and it tears me apart even worse now that she's gone. Maybe if I would have accepted her back and did more to make our marriage work, then maybe this wouldn't have happened. Nelle makes her own decisions, I know, but on some hundred talk, I never stopped lovin' Nelle one bit.

The lobby is packed with Nelle's family and friends mourning her loss. No one knew that her problem had become that bad. Although they did know that she done a few pills, liquor, and occasionally took a puff or two of a blunt. The doctors said she had to have taken at least thirty of them from the blood sample that they took from her.

I can't believe this bull, I say to myself while thinkin' bout all the things that me and Nelle been through. I can't help but remember Nelle being my baby, my heart and soul. When we first met, we were inseparable. You would have thought that we would have been together forever or until death done us apart. It's crazy that instill, death did do us apart, but this soon, in this type a way, I never would have imagined.

Chapter Thirty-Six

Now that I have my kids' fulltime I'm through with all the runnin' around nonsense. It's strictly family first.

And business of course.

"J3," I said as I heard his voice on the other end of the phone. "I been doin' some thinkin' and I'm gone back off of Skinz for a lil' bit and all the Yung Ruff momentum and live a new life. A changed life. A life for Christ. Cross life."

"Bro," J3 said. "I'm down with whatever you tryna do, because I know it's all good. Even though I'm the big brother and I'll still whoop yo' lil' butt like I use to when we was kids. You are kind of smart when it comes to business ways."

"Bro, let's sell the club and use the profit to do something else. We've already made our money in it. It can still stay open but under new management because we are sellin' the buyers all of it."

"Charles, we got enough money anyways, so however you want to do it, let's do it."

"Thanks bro. I will get back wit' you later." I hang up the phone. To my surprise, the phone starts ringin' again as I'm sittin' on the porch getting a breeze and watching traffic. It's Prophet Joseph-Israel. "Hello, Brother Franck," I say.

"How you doin' Brother Ruffin?"

"It's good to hear from you."

"I have not forgotten about you one bit. In fact, God has put it on my heart to give you a hand. I heard through your sister that you've been goin' through changes and I heard about your wife. I'm sorry. I want you to know, brother, that you have a place here in Maryland with me so that you can have a fresh start away from the Oklahoma lifestyle of drugs and gangs. I know how much you want to do right, but still have your struggles. Let me remind you that no matter where you go, if you're not really ready to change, you'll do the same thing wherever you go. As long as God wills and allows, I'm here to help you in whatever areas; as your pastor, mentor, and friend."

"I appreciate it sincerely, Brother and am glad that you called. I had just hung up the phone with my brother telling him that I'm through with the worldly lifestyle and all the clubbin' and drugs and secular music—which I've been doin' fairly well in. I realize if I continue to do that same music then I'm gone keep on putting myself in the club scenes, drug scenes and lustful situations. Not to mention, that you never know what will transpire in a club scene."

"I understand. How are the kids?"

"They're doing fine," I said. "They're still a little shook up from Nelle passing away but besides that, they're being some terrific kids. I couldn't ask for some kids who are more well-mannered than them."

"I know it will be a huge change moving up here to Maryland, but you and the kids will love it. In fact, we have one of the best school systems in the whole wide world."

"Well Brother Franck, I'm all the way down with making a move because I have got to get myself all the way together. I'm sad to say that moving from Muskogee to Tulsa was not good enough so Maryland here I come. Give me about a week or so to let all my family know as well as the kids and then we will go from there."

"Okay!" Prophet Joseph Israel said. "Also know that you don't have to worry about housing because I have a few real estate houses that God has blessed me with and in return I will bless you and your kids. Believe me, it's nice, brother. Also please don't call me Brother Franck no more because he is a dead man never to return. I know you don't mean anything bad by saying that but I left him a long time ago brother."

"Okay I gotcha Brother! You know I got nothing but respect for you. Thanks again," I say. "I'm thankful to be able to have this opportunity to start anew. I sincerely appreciate this."

"All glory to God. I will help keep you up lifted in prayer like I have been doing. I love you brother and if there's anything else that you need then feel free to let me know. You can call me anytime. If I don't answer, then leave me a voicemail and I will return the call."

"Alrighty then, I love ya Brother and God bless."

"God bless you, too."

As I hang up the phone, I begin thinkin' how things will be in Maryland which is the East Coast. I don't know exactly, but it's gotta be better than Oklahoma. At least for me it should be, because I have a new start. Nobody will know me and I won't know nobody either. In a way, that's a good thing but then again it brings me some anxiety of the unknown but I'm down with it.

It's crazy how Prophet Joseph Israel called out the blue and was sayin' what he said and I was *already* thinkin' the same. I need a change of scenery. I know there is no such thing as coincidence, so God had to really put it on his heart that I'm tryna get myself together cause I ain't heard from him in a cool minute. God is real and He works in mysterious ways.

"Brother Franck is a dead man never to return", I laugh. "I can dig that."

Chapter Thirty-Seven

I'm tired of talkin' the talk and not walkin' the walk. I've given it all to God and I'm walkin' into a new life. For He says in His Word in 2nd Corinthians 5:17, "Therefore, if any man be in Christ, he is a new creature. Old things have passed away. Behold, all things are made new."

I claim victory right now and am choosing this day to no longer be a victim. I've told my momma and sisters and brother and the rest of my family and friends that I will be leaving out to start anew in Germantown, Maryland. They don't want me to go but they're all for it because they know it's what's best for me. My kids are excited about going though.

I'm tired of this no good game in which I knew from the start wasn't nothin' but a shame. I'm through with living for myself. I'ma live for Jesus from this day forward. I'm through with the lip service. I have given it all to Jesus whom said to me in Isaiah 43:18-19, "Forget the former things, do not dwell on the past. For I am doing a new thing. Now that it springs up, do you not perceive it? I am making a way in the desert and streams in the wasteland."

I've wasted enough time and have no more time to waste. I'm sick and tired of fallin' victim to this shame game. Therefore, I've made a conscious decision while I'm out here on these streets and still have life in me to make a complete change. The old me is dead and I'ma let em stay dead in the Name of Jesus. That's why I feel Prophet Joseph Israel on the name change. Cross life is back and back to stay for good.

Right now, I feel more motivated than ever to be a success in life. I know I've made many mistakes and wrong decisions but I also know that the past cannot be brought back. I now look forward to a brighter future.

As I look back at the game, I've had some good times but I've also had lots of bad miserable days in the game. It seems like yesterday I was in a jail cell making change in life. I know I fell back victim to the streets of chasing money, women, and the fast life, but I now realize that the price to pay is not worth the risk.

A new life I will live and show my kids the way to live as productive citizens in society. I will never forget their mother Nelle, whom was truly the love of my heart. I know we both had our childish ways at times, but what ghetto love story doesn't? My homeboy JoJo will never be forgotten and none of my true people in this game will be either. But for me, I have got to do what's best for me and mine, and that's to change and get up out this dirty game. The game aint nothin' but a shame and if you aint know then now you know.

Cross life for Christ. The journey begins. Ima bout to go from affliction to benediction in the name of Jesus.

Germantown, Maryland here I come!

Made in the USA
Coppell, TX
24 February 2021